UNVEILING ALICE

UNVEILING ALICE

ALICE

MARY CROCKER

NEW DEGREE PRESS

UNVEILING ALICE

ISBN   978-1-63730-801-1   *Paperback*

         978-1-63730-860-8   *Kindle Ebook*

         978-1-63730-987-2   *Ebook*

To my mom, Carla, and my grandma Alice,
the two strongest women I know.

Your example made this comeback possible.

Contents

Chapter One

———

My curler and hairspray make contact as I wrap my last strand of hair around the iron.

Sizzzzzle.

The bathroom feels exceptionally warm as my body continues to cool down from my morning workout. As I start to unravel my curl, I see David's head peer to the right and make eye contact with me in the mirror from the kitchen counter.

Oh, the thrill of sharing a small space.

"Babe, are those the jeans I got you for your birthday? Or are those *another* new pair?" David asks from the other room.

"No, hun, these are old," I say, hiding my eye roll, "but clearly they caught your attention, huh?"

"They did, but also wanted to make sure we aren't spending unnecessary money."

Not this morning, David, please. Not the week of our wedding.

"All I hear is that you like them on me," I say, turning back to him with a playful smile.

He knows how much I cringe at those types of questions because it's his not-so-passive way of asking if I've been shopping. Wedding planning causes so many headaches and brings unnecessary tensions over finances. Especially when your fiancé is the king of budgeting and saving.

"I won't deny that," he says, making his way to me as I shake out the curls in my hair. "Love them on you so much. I don't know if I want anyone else to see you wearing them."

There he is. Back to the man who just wants me all to himself. My heart could not be more ready for our next chapter. I'm ready for the wedding planning to be done and to say I do to forever.

"Oh shush, you know you have me," I say, pulling him into me. "And in just a matter of days, you'll have me all to yourself. Forever."

Ping ping. My phone goes off, and I see emails firing in from work.

"Sorry, hun, I need to finish getting ready." I turn back to the mirror to do my makeup.

But David isn't having that answer. He follows my movements back to the counter and softly kisses my neck while wrapping his arms around me.

"I can't help it."

"Well, you're going to have to. One more day until I'm all yours and free from work—"

"Until the wedding is over..."

"David, please."

"I know, I know. You love work. It gives you purpose, fuels your passions," he subtly mocks my words. "Anyways, how was your workout? You're looking good," he changes the subject.

"Workout was great," I say, applying my mascara. "Crushed some weights and hammered it home with some cardio, as per usual. Oh, I also listened to an interesting podcast. They dove into the benefits of collagen and how important vitamins are. Which reminds me, I just ordered some, and they'll be delivered here in a few weeks."

"You got it." He is still standing next to me.

"Hey, you good?" I turn to him.

"Yeah, why?"

"I don't know. You seem different this morning, that's all," I say, looking up at him. Gosh, I will never get over David's height. Good looks, successful, and tall. I guess you *can* have it all.

"All good—" My phone notifications are still buzzing.

"Sorry," I say, trying my best to ignore it.

"Busy girl," he responds. "You know you don't have to work so much. It's not as if you'll need to work forever, remember?"

Doing my best to stay cool, I try to figure out what is up with him this morning. He's touchy but cold.

"Hun, look, I know we talked about that, but I want to excel at this new role and embrace my career as much as I can for now, okay?" I cup his face in my hands. "Just be excited with me. Please."

"I am... I am..." David says in return, but it doesn't feel convincing. Not as convincing as the sudden kiss that follows. Within seconds, I'm in his arms bridal style and set on the kitchen counter. Our kiss is heated and distracting. So much so that my hand sends a warm coffee cup too close to the edge.

"David!" I squeal out. "Careful!"

But he laughs and continues to engage. While my body is craving some early morning fun, my mind is on the meeting I have first thing at the office.

"David, I have to go," I say, pulling back and bringing my shirt down. "And you should get back to work too."

"C'mon, you can be a little late," He reaches for my shirt again. "It's just a trendy tech company. Your team plays ping pong more than you do actual work."

Choosing to dismiss the comment, I say, "Hun, I am serious. I have a meeting. I have to go." I am more assertive in my movements as I jump off the counter.

He turns away from me without a saying word and goes back to his desk. As much as I want to give in and give him what he wants this morning, I have to get to work. This promotion was huge. After working with the company for ten months, the Marketing Manager position opened up, and it was an offer I could not refuse. My own office, a team to lead, and a killer salary.

We could buy a home. Start a family. David will see the fruition of my career one day. It's what we both want.

"Where are my brown heels?" I yell from the closet.

"Look on the top shelf," David responds.

"Great, I wanted to be there a little early." I rush back to the kitchen, "Can you help me hook this necklace?"

"Alice, you don't always have to get so dressed up for work."

"Yes, I do. Big girl job means big girl attire," I say, turning back to face him. "Which reminds me, I need to run to Costco after work today. Need a few crucial lady items. Can we go after work?"

"Um, maybe." He draws me in closer. "Can I let you know later today?"

I know where this is headed once again.

"Sure, let me know. I have to go now. I love you." I leave him with a kiss.

But David doesn't just kiss me back lightly. His hands are wrapped in my hair, and his lips are locked; his affection is intense.

"You are something else this morning," I say, teasing him. "Save this for the 'I do's this weekend."

"Alice," he pauses, holding me close in his arms, "I love you too."

"You make saying goodbye so hard, but I *really* do have to get to work."

I can feel his disappointment when his shoulders drop. David is successful and makes enough money for us to live comfortably. His job has not brought him the same level of excitement mine has given me. If it were up to him, I'd be home, training to be a stay-at-home mom.

"No, I get it. You should go. Have a good day," he says, leaving me with one more gentle kiss.

*

Thankfully the drive to work is easy. Traffic is bearable, and I make it in time to review notes before the first meeting kicks off. After my third meeting of the morning, I finally get a moment to myself.

Me: *Hey hun, how is the morning going?*

David: *Just a few emails, nothing exciting. I'm actually trying to figure out this new program my boss tasked me with.*

Me: *I'm sorry, hun, but at least it is something new to work on!*

Bubbles linger, but he gives me no response.

Me: *Oh my goodness, the funniest thing happened in our team meeting this morning. I can't wait to tell you about it. Also, my boss loved the idea about starting PR boxes. I feel like everything is finally aligning. Just in time before we get married. How amazing is that?*

David: *Cool!*

David: *By the way, let's go to Costco after work. I will meet you there.*

Me: *Sure you don't want to ride together? I can pick you up after work?*

David: *No, it's fine.*

Me: *Oh yay! You are* the *best, can't wait. Counting down the hours until the workday is over!*

David: *Would you be up for a walk as well? We could just go on the trail that runs behind Costco.*

Me: **Duh!** *I would love nothing more my soon-to-be husband. Got to run, emails are firing off. Love you! XO*

*

No airport has ever looked and felt like such a blur, and I have traveled at some ungodly hours in my past.

The tears clouding my vision, snot dripping from my nose, and nauseating pain in my stomach is making it hard to focus. Two suitcases and a carry-on seemed like the right decision two hours ago.

But now, I am frustrated, scared, and sweating from the weight of everything.

Of course, today, of all days, the elevator is out of service. So help me, if I have to manage these suitcases up one more escalator, I will scream. More so than I did on my drive here. To make it worse, every person I pass takes a second look at me. And not the good of kind of second look. Can people please give me space?

With no time or thought to change, my outfit feels stiff, and these heels are not suitable for racing through an airport. Normally I would never travel like this, but I didn't have a choice. I booked the last flight of the day and had to rush my way through an hour of traffic to get here. Time was of the essence to get on the road. And these jeans, these stupid, stupid jeans. Honestly, I only kept them because David liked them on me, but now they feel tight and uncomfortable. Gosh, I don't even want to be in my own skin right now. Anything to escape this moment. This undeniably embarrassing walk of shame through the airport. I am the walking definition of a hot mess. My flesh is on fire. I can't catch my breath or stop myself from shaking as I make my way to the bag drop-off.

Can you people please stop staring? I have a plane to catch here like the rest of you. Mind your own business. The last thing I need is to miss a flight and be stuck in this state.

"Hello, ma'am, go ahead and place both suitcases up on the scale," the employee behind the counter greets me.

Both of us bring our attention to the 106 pounds lighting up the scale. Six pounds over, but I don't care. Let me pay and be on my way today.

"Ma'am," he stops me as I reach for my wallet. "Don't worry about it."

"Are… Are you sure?" I'm still fishing for my wallet.

"Absolutely. It's on us today. Your flight boards soon, so you should get going. Have a safe trip." His tone is genuine and compassionate. Qualities I wish someone could have given me earlier today.

Racing through TSA, I can feel the eyes of strangers watching my every move. This is not the kind of attention I was hoping to receive during my wedding week. I've been dreaming up compliments, gifts, admiration, and adoration from others.

People are clearing out of my way and offering me gentle nods. Normally I wouldn't despise people for their sympathy, but right now, I do. I want to be alone. I want to just get to my seat and curl up in a ball and be left to myself to cry.

Waiting for the tram to arrive and take me to my gate, I brave checking my phone—twenty-three unread text messages.

Mom: *Dad and I are on our way to Burbank airport. Keep us posted. We love you.*

Devon: *Alice, I am so sorry. I love you. Text me when you land.*

William: *Screw him. What an idiot. We love you, Alice. We are here for you.*

Lizzie: *I'm so sorry this is happening. Let me know what you need. Praying for you, sis. I love you.*

Mitchell: *Stay strong. Tell us what you need. We are here for you. Love you.*

JulieAnn: *Did you make it okay? Hate that you drove to the airport all alone in a state like this. Who lets their fiancée drive in such an emotional state?* Unacceptable. *Where is this coming from? I love you, though. I'm so sorry.*

Not a single text from David. While I appreciate the "I love you's" from my family, all I want right now is to feel his embrace. Just the one from this morning. I want to feel David's love. It's all I've ever wanted. He put a ring on my finger. We dreamed up a future together. I believed he loved me. I thought he loved me.

Making it to my gate with about ten minutes to spare, I rush to make a sad attempt at freshening up in the bathroom. Although, I don't think anything will really help at this point. I'm hopeless. I look in the mirror, and the pain pierces through my stomach.

Who is this girl? How did I get here? How did we get here? What in the actual heck just happened?

This is not the ending I envisioned. I've heard stories like this about other people. Maybe even in a movie. But it's not supposed to happen to me.

"Do you need a tissue?" a voice beside me offers over a small pack of Kleenex.

"Oh, thank you." I reach to grab one. "Appreciate it."

"Here, take the pack. I always carry extras." She leaves me with them and heads out.

So the pity begins. This can't be real. How am I supposed to go out and face the world?

Splashing some water on my face, I feel my body cool down for the first time since arriving. I let the water sit on my face for a second longer before patting it dry. My gate is right outside the restroom, so I decide to wait until the very last minute for boarding. At this point, I've had enough unwanted attention from strangers. I want to walk out and right onto the plane.

As I walk up to my gate, I notice there isn't a large crowd waiting to board. Hopefully means I can score a row to myself. Making my way to the line, I see an outfit on a woman that looks oddly familiar. Green linen joggers and white peasant blouse paired perfectly with Golden Goose sneakers. Fabulous travel outfit, but why does it...

Oh shoot, I know that person.

Holli, my dear Holli. It's her. We worked closely for several years at Anthropologie. She is a fashion inspiration anywhere she goes, and it's now dawning on me that I saw her outfit during my aimless Instagram scrolling at lunch today.

But, no, not now. I love her, but not now. No, she cannot see me this way. Where can I go? Scanning my surroundings as the flight attendant announces, "*Now boarding Group A for Flight 1382 to Burbank, California.*"

Ugh!

My body freezes, and I hope she won't see me. It's been a few years, so I've changed a little. My hair is longer. I wear glasses. That has to be enough of a disguise, right?

Although my staring must have caught her attention.

"Alice? What? Is that really you? Oh my gosh, Alice! Johnny look," she cries, nudging her husband, "it's Alice!"

Her voice is loud and draws the eyes of people away from their phones to our interaction.

"Alice, come here," she says, waving her hand at me. "I can't believe it's you!"

Out of all the times I have flown, today is the day I'm seeing someone I know? God help me.

Making my way to her, I do my best to smile. I even use my hands to signal she needs to lower her voice.

"Alice!" she cries, immediately pulling me in for a hug, "What are you doing here? And look at you! You... You have glasses now. Wow! And your hair; it's longer."

This woman. Her attention to detail is almost scary. But I can sense she is doing her best to point out everything about me except the tears filling my eyes once again.

"Hey Holli, so good to see you," is all I can muster out right now.

"Alice, how are you? Aren't you getting married soon? Why are you going home now so close to the wedding? Did something happen in your family? Is everything okay?"

The questions overwhelm me. I'm trying not to make a scene, but I can't quite find the right words. Where do I even begin?

"No, um... My family is great, just fine."

"So why are you going home alone?" Her voice starts to lower. "Where is your fiancé? I've only seen him on Instagram. Can I finally meet the man in real life? It's David, right?"

His name. My eyes are welling up, and I'm doing my best to get words out, but my body is physically incapable. I've lost all control.

Holli's husband, Johnny, has taken notice that something is definitely wrong and turns to give us our space. My head falls. I would do anything not to deal with this in public.

"Alice, what happened?" She's searching my eyes for an explanation. "You're scaring me."

"Holli, I, um... I just need to go home for a bit."

Why is telling the truth so hard? Why can't I get the words out?

"Okay." Talking slowly and grabbing my hand as we walk up closer to the gate, she says, "But why are you alone?"

I can feel her ginormous diamond wedding ring against my skin. Makes me even sicker.

"David, um... He is staying here in Colorado while I go."

"Alice, I'm sorry, I don't mean to pry, but I don't understand. Why wouldn't he come with you? I thought your wedding was coming up?"

Deep breath. Hold it together, Alice. You're almost on the plane.

"Holli, I'm not... I'm not getting married any time soon."

"What do you mean? You *just* posted about it last night, counting down the days to your ceremony. Why did you have to push it back?"

She has so many questions, and I don't blame her. I would be just as confused if I saw myself in this state after all the posts I have filled my Instagram feed with. Another embarrassing reminder to delete those and eat my words.

"No, Holli, I'm not—" I'm pinching my eyes, my body shaking uncontrollably.

"Alice, don't tell me..." Holli's face goes blank.

Tears fall. Loud, big, drastic tears for everyone to see and hear.

"David," I'm barely able to say his name, "doesn't want to marry me anymore."

Chapter Two

Before Holli can bring herself to speak, a flight announcement blares over the intercom.

"Guests of today's flight to Burbank, please make sure to line up accordingly to your boarding number and have your boarding pass out to be scanned."

The confusion on her face switches to pity. I hate it.

"What? What do you... What does he... What does 'not getting married anymore' mean?" Holli asks.

"I don't know, Holli, he just doesn't want me, he wants—" I'm hit with the painful memory of what David said hours ago. Within minutes, our future together fell apart.

"Oh, Alice, come here," Holli pulls me in for a hug, "Okay, look, I have to board now, but we will save you a spot."

I step aside so others can board. Why is it that I was the one who got dumped, yet I feel horrible delivering this news? I didn't cause this heartache; David did, but sharing with people is excruciating. It's humiliating.

The man I talked to this afternoon was not my David. I have no clue who that man was. He went from being my soon-to-be husband, my everything, the center of my world, to an absolute stranger. Nothing felt real this afternoon.

As I wait to board, I decide to sift through the endless texts from my family. A few have even asked if they could reach out to David. There's no point. If I couldn't change his mind, they certainly won't. No amount of begging could get that man to take back his words. And seeing what he did to me this afternoon, I can't begin to think how he might treat my family.

Everyone's eyes land on me as we wait to board our flight. I keep my head down while tears continue to fall. More texts ping in. Surely he has to reach out and make sure I made it here safely.

Maybe when I land. Give it time, Alice.

When I make my way onto the plane, I see Holli perched in the front row, with her husband Johnny in the row beside us.

"Alice, here you go," she says, tapping the seat next to her, which already has tissues and a water waiting for me.

"Thank you," I say to her and Johnny, who clearly gave up his spot for me to sit next to her.

"Alice, I can't believe we are on the same flight going home. Do you have a ride when you get there? Johnny and I can take you home or help you get a hotel," Holli offers, and before I can answer, she continues. "Alice, how did this happen? I'm sorry, I know I cut you off, but I am so lost... It's just that you two looked so in love. What an idiot. What happened?"

"I have a ride from my parents. Thanks, though," I say, avoiding the other questions as I open my water.

"Do they know why you're coming home? How did this all happen? I mean, your wedding is *days* away."

"They know he ended it. That's all."

While the flight attendants go over the safety protocols, I think about how my family was getting ready to come to Colorado for the wedding. This is pathetic. Now I am going home single, lost, and broken. Absolutely shattered.

"Why, though, Alice? Why did he do this?" I feel Holli pick up my hand. "And where is your ring. Alice, tell me right now you have the ring. You did not give that stupid man back the diamond."

"I—I left it there. I couldn't stand to wear it," I shamefully admit. "People would think I'm engaged. He doesn't want the actual me, so what's the point?"

"Well, I can't believe he kept it after doing this. Says more about him than you—"

"Does it? Feels like there is more wrong with me."

"No! Nothing is wrong with you!" Holli snaps back.

"He was perfect, Holli, and I wasn't good enough for him—"

"No one is perfect, and no relationship is perfect. You can't beat yourself up over his dumb decision. But Alice, you have to get that ring back. It is yours to keep. Don't let that man keep it—no way."

"What does it matter, Holli? He doesn't want to marry me," I say, my head falling back on my seat, replaying the scene in my mind. "He just ended it. Like it was nothing. Like I was nothing."

"But did he say why?"

"He gave a reason or two, but Holli, it's nothing that you end an engagement over. And it doesn't matter. He was practically my husband. My whole future—everything—is just gone. What do I do?"

"Alice, this doesn't make sense. I don't understand. No one just leaves for no reason. There has to be something."

"I wish I understood. I thought he loved me." These words hit me hard. How stupid I must sound saying this about a man who left me.

"Well, have you heard from him? Maybe he just got cold feet? That happened to Carrie and Big on *Sex in the City*, remember? They worked it out. This can't be the end for you two. You looked so happy."

This reference makes me chuckle. Only Holli would find a way to make a *Sex and the City* reference during this time. It was the release of tension we both needed.

"No, I haven't heard from him. We're over. I saw it in him. He was done." Looking down as I pick at my fingers, I say, "Holli, how will I get through this?"

"Alice, you will get through it. It will be hard, but you will—day by day. Alice, you are strong. Don't lose that spirit and spark that is in you. Just because David failed to hold onto it doesn't mean you should."

"Thank you. I want this pain to go away. Will I ever fully get over it?"

"That's the thing about grief: you don't know. And it's honestly too early to even tell how you'll respond. Healing isn't linear, and this will be a part of your story for the rest of your life. The bright side is that *you* have the power to choose what you will make of it, not him."

My head rests back on the seat, thinking about what Holli said. I need to get home. My head is pounding with the worst headache, and I can't help but think about the long drive home from the airport.

"Alice, I do have to ask," Holli interrupts my thoughts and rest. "He didn't end it because he was, you know—"

"What?" I say, grinning back at her.

"Gay?" she whispers so softly. It makes me laugh.

First, the *Sex in the City* reference and now this. Only Holli. She is trying hard to be sensitive to my situation and the people around us.

"Gosh, I almost wish. It would make this easier to understand," I say, sighing. "But no. Quite the opposite, actually."

"Oh good, so the sex was good then? This wasn't a Charlotte from *Sex and the City* situation, was it?"

"You and that show. The references are endless," I laugh. "But no. We actually were waiting until marriage." I brace for her response and feel guilty about disclosing our intimate life. David and I were always very private about this area of our relationship.

"*What!* No sex?" Holli responds much louder than the way she whispered moments ago.

"Shhh, Holli! People can hear you."

"Good, they should. Wow, I mean, well, wow. I respect your decision, but I mean, how did you manage that? Shoot, how did he manage that?"

"It was what we decided. Well, maybe more so what *he* decided. You know how important my faith is to me, and I loved him. It felt right."

Why am I defending him or our relationship?

"So wait, is he a," her whispering is back, "*you know.* Not having had sex."

"Yes, yes he is."

"But you're not, right?"

"Okay, you're cut off," I say, laughing. "I'm sorry, but can we please change the subject?"

"Yes, I'm sorry."

"It's okay. I just need to get my mind off this topic for a bit."

"Okay, I am done with my questions now. Let's talk fashion. I want to show you these shoes I want! How do we feel about bright pink booties?"

And just like that, we are two friends talking fashion as if nothing has changed. As if we haven't gone two years without seeing each other. As if four hours ago, my future didn't just take a traumatic turn. I take a moment to soak in Holli's sweet spirit and thank God for sending this angel. What state would I have been in if I had to spend two hours on a late-night flight alone?

Alone. The word sends chills down my back. From engaged to alone in a matter of minutes.

*

"We are starting our descent into Burbank, California. Weather is currently 78 degrees, and the local time is 11:10 p.m."

We must be the last flight to land because it's a ghost town. Holli and Johnny say their goodbyes to me so I can have my space with my parents when I get to baggage claim. My heart is racing as fast as my feet. I'm on the verge of running to get to my parents.

The sliding doors open, and I look to my right. My parents are there, ready as ever. My duffel bag drops to the ground, and my legs lock up. Frozen, I let them make their way toward me. Tears start falling before they can even reach me.

"Alice, I'm so, so sorry." My mom is struggling to speak.

"Alice, I—" My dad hugs me next. "I'm so sorry."

The hugs are long, neither of them wanting to let go. This is so much more painful than I expected. I hate to see them cry and know I'm the reason behind it.

"How was the flight? How are you? What do you need?" My mom clutches my arm tight.

It's one thing to deal with your own pain, but to watch your parents hurt by your suffering, is a whole other degree of guilt. They wouldn't be crying if it weren't for my failed engagement. They wouldn't have had to drop everything at the drop of a hat to drive hours to come pick me up. My parents shouldn't be the ones dealing with this, though, but I didn't know who else to call. It's my problem, my brokenness, my shame, my fault—not theirs.

"Just need my bags. And some Tylenol."

Mom is already digging through her purse. "I couldn't believe your text that Holli was on your flight," she says while handing me a few capsules.

"Right? Crazy. Thankful I had her with me," I say, watching the bags circulate on the belt. "I'm so sorry you two had to come."

"Don't be. Of course, we're here," my dad says. "I can't believe he did this."

"We're so happy you called us and decided to come home," my mom shares.

My bags finally come out, and my dad insists on carrying all my luggage. The walk back to the car is pretty silent. No one knows what to say or do. I pull out my phone and scroll through the several text messages from Devon, Holli, and my siblings. But nothing from David.

Does he really just not care?

"So, how did you get to the airport?" my mom kicks off the small talk. "Where did you leave your car?"

"I drove. My car is at the airport."

"Wait, you drove all by yourself?" my dad asks. "David let you drive all by yourself?"

"Yes." My answer is short. I'm hesitant to reveal too much. I don't want my parents to start ripping into David. "It's okay. I made that choice, and I'll deal with the airport parking costs another time."

"Alice, he should not have let you drive alone. That is not okay," my mom's tone is disappointing.

"Well, I'm here. It's fine."

Mom breaks my silence again, "Alice, I know it's late, but would you be okay telling us what happened?"

My mouth opens, but words don't follow so easily. Where do I even start when I don't have all the answers myself?

"I really wish I understood. It was a normal day, a great morning, actually." Struggling to finish my answer, I say, "and then suddenly it was over."

"So he didn't offer a reason?" my dad asks.

"No, I mean, he gave a reason or two. But nothing that made sense. He just doesn't want me anymore." I'm barely holding myself together as the words leave my mouth.

"No, not an acceptable answer," the anger is evident in my dad. "No one can call off a wedding like this and leave someone this confused. A real man doesn't do that."

"Well, he did..." I respond.

"I'm sorry, but I gave him my blessing to take your hand in marriage, and now he does this? You don't go back on your word like that."

"Dad, it's not worth it." I cut him off before anything hurtful about David is said.

"Alice, you're my daughter. This is bullshit. I hate seeing you like this. What a coward. Leaving you like this, not taking care of you—"

"I know, Dad," I say, interrupting him, "but it's done."

My mom puts her hand on my dad's arm to cool him down. "Alice, we are so thankful you texted us. This is what we are here for. You won't be alone to get through this."

Keeping my head rested on the window, I look out and watch the cars passing by on the freeway. It's dark, it's late, and I'm exhausted. I can't help but glance down at my phone again. Still no text or missed call from David. What could he be doing right now? How has he not reached out to me?

Why is the person who hurt me the most the only one I want beside me right now?

*

Three hours later, I'm back in my childhood home; a place of comfort. The smell hasn't changed. The same wallpaper covers the walls. Photos fill the fridge. Old newspaper articles from our sports days crowd the bulletin board. Even the stack of mail sits in the same corner on the kitchen counter.

Ironic how little has changed here in comparison to my life.

Looking in the bathroom mirror, I don't recognize the girl in front of me. Her face is blotchy red, eyes puffed, and shoulders slumped. It's sad. It's depressing. I don't even bother with my full skincare routine tonight. What's the point anymore? I'm not prepping for the most photographed day in my life anymore. No need to bother maintaining the work of expensive prewedding facials.

When I go back into my room, I pull out my pajamas and yell out to my parents, "Thank you again. Good night."

"Good night, Alice, we love you. If you need anything—" they respond.

"I know, thank you. Love you guys," I say, cutting them off as I shut my door. It's 2 a.m., and my eyes are barely staying open, but I'm anxious to get under the covers.

Everything hits hard.

My body is aching. Every inch of my skin. Uncomfortable, throbbing, desperate for something to take it away. Almost as if I have been physically beaten down to the point of no return. I curl into the tightest position possible, holding my knees close to my chest. My body is craving to be held, longing to be wrapped. I'm doing my best to keep it together, but my tears turn into sobbing.

Shit. This hurts.

David, I need you. You're all I want right now.

Chapter Three

My body may be living in a different time zone, but that isn't what wakes me so early. The pounding in my head is excruciating. Not even my worst college hangover did this kind of damage. My head feels heavy, filled with pressure and intense throbbing. As I lie on my back, I lift my left hand in the air and see my ring finger is still empty.

What happened yesterday was actually real and not a horrible nightmare. How am I going to face the world?

The news is playing outside my room, and I'm sure my mom is waiting for me to come out. But right now, I am numb and want to be left alone. I don't have any reason to get up, and my body feels glued to the bed. Numb yet filled with aches at the same time. How is it possible to feel this broken?

Ping ping.

My body suddenly finds the strength to move at the sound of my phone. This must be David.

But it's not. Instead, I see our premarital counselor's name pop up.

Hmm, that's odd. What would Ann be texting me about so early?

Ann: ***Oh Alice, I wish I could give you a hug. I am so sorry. Please know that we are praying for you and are here if you need anything.***

Um... Excuse me?

What is happening? I've been home for *maybe* seven hours. Barely awake for ten minutes. And David already told our premarital counselors? He really is done with me. Done with our relationship. Otherwise, he wouldn't be telling people within less than twenty-four hours that our wedding is called off. Especially people who weren't even invited to the wedding.

I throw my phone off my bed, wanting it as far away from me as possible as I turn my body back onto my stomach and push my face into the pillow. I can't already be crying again.

What is my life right now?

Knock knock.

Seriously? I'm not ready to talk to anyone. Maybe coming home was the wrong idea. I know my parents mean well, but I want to cry alone. They saw enough last night. I use my shirt to wipe underneath my eyes and use my wrist to wipe away any lingering snot. I can't let them think I woke up like this.

"Come in," I say softly.

To my surprise, it's not my mom. It's one of my brothers, Nate. He cracks the door open, and I can see he is dressed for work. What is doing here then?

"Hey," he says gently.

"Hey." I'm barely able to look up at him.

"How are you doing?"

"Well, you know," I sigh, "I have seen better days."

"You know, I was thinking the same thing, but those are your words, not mine." We both share a laugh. "Can I come in?"

He sits on the edge of my bed, and before he says anything, he pulls me in for a hug. My arms don't even make their way around him before the tears start. My head falls onto his shoulder as he holds me tight. Neither of us says a word.

"I'm so sorry, Alice," Nate finally breaks the silence.

"Nate, don't cry, you didn't—" My heart is breaking. First my parents, now my brother. This isn't right.

"No, Alice, I'm sorry. This situation; it shouldn't happen to people like you. You deserve better. And I'm sorry I didn't call last night. I wasn't sure what to say."

"Thank you. It's okay. I don't really know what to say either."

"I do know that I want to kind of want to kick his ass, though." He gives a quick air punch. "Just a quick one-two punch."

Again I'm laughing. I could have done without the tears, but this I needed.

"No, no, that won't be necessary."

"Alice, how could he do this to you? We all trusted him when we welcomed him to the family. This is unforgivable. He better never try to show his face here again."

"I really don't know. I don't know what went wrong. Everything was fine, and then suddenly it wasn't. Trust me, I tried to change his mind, but there was nothing I could do—"

"Change his mind? No. You should marry someone who has no doubt in their mind that you're the best thing to happen to them."

"Yeah..."

This is really all I can get out of me right now.

"Is there anything I can grab for you before I head out?" Nate asks.

"No, it's okay. But really, thank you for coming over. I'm sorry you have to see me like this—"

"Don't say sorry. You're not the one who needs to apologize. David should and will be sorry he did this," he says while grabbing a tissue from the box my mom left me with last night. I can count on one hand how many times I've seen my brother cry.

"I don't look like I cried, right?" He pulls his shoulders back and wipes his eyes. "I don't want anyone to know. Secret stays here. You got it?"

"You got it," I'm laughing at his ridiculous attempt to try and stay tough. Underneath Nate's shell of humor and masculinity is a compassionate, empathetic soul.

Once the door shuts, I fall back into bed and continue to cry. How is it that my brother was able to console me, but David couldn't? My own fiancé left me on my knees in that apartment. Crying in the closet as I ripped clothes off the hangers and packed.

David couldn't even shed a single tear.

*

After Nate left, I fell back asleep, but I was once again awoken by my headache. I force myself out of bed and grab my phone. As I get up, I realize how badly I need to use the restroom, which means I will have to leave my room. My phone lights up. So many text messages, and not just from people checking in on me. I see several names of wedding vendors.

Ugh. I forgot I have a wedding to un-plan.

The house is quiet, and the tile floor feels cold. My mom is on the couch with her laptop, and I do my best not to acknowledge her head popping up as I walk to the bathroom. I can feel her ready to talk and ask questions.

"Good morning!" she yells out right as I close the bathroom door.

Mirrors are really starting to become my least favorite household item. They unveil the terrifying reality of what I am living. My eyes are still puffy and bloodshot red, so much so that I don't even bother with my contacts. Although, I do take a moment to wash my face and clean up. As I brush my teeth, I check my phone. Habit of trying to kill two birds with one stone.

Fifteen unread messages and still not a single one from David.

My wedding coordinator: *Alice! Checking in to see if there is anything I can do before the big day. So excited to see you in that dress. David doesn't know what is coming! Can't wait for the day to be here. Counting down!*

Oh, and I emailed you a final itinerary. Let me know if I missed anything!

My wedding photographer: *Thinking of you two gorgeous people today! I can't wait to photograph the actual day! Let me know if there is anything I need to know or bring! Can't wait!*

My brushing comes to a stop as I stare at a photo of David and I. We do photograph *so* well together, and David is so handsome. I can't help but reminisce on the very moment this photo was taken. Our hands locked together, facing one another, both of us smiling so wide. He's leaning down to me as I stand on my tippy toes.

Gosh, I love how tall he is.

During this particular photo moment, our wedding photographer told David to whisper something in my ear. And I lost it when he said, "*I can't wait to take you home after our wedding and rip your dress off you. Let's just go get married already.*"

This was so out of character for him to tease like that with another person around. So I was not only stunned but also completely enchanted with the man entangled in my hands. My face glowed, thinking about our wedding night.

Our engagement shoot was one of my favorite days. David was playful and flirty during our session: lifting me up, squeezing my bottom, kissing me endlessly, dancing with me. The photos were stunning. Now they're reminders of what never came to be. My eyes slowly start welling up, so I close out of the photo, finish brushing my teeth, and open a text from Holli.

Holli: *Hi Alice, how are you doing? Thinking of you and sending you the biggest hug today. Remember what we talked about on the plane: take care of Alice, focus on you. Drink water, wash your face, go for a walk, and journal. Sending you my love.*

I still can't believe I saw her last night. What a gift and a nightmare having to face people so soon.

"How are you feeling?" my mom asks as I head toward the couch. She closes her computer and sits upright, turning to me like she is ready to chat. But I'm not.

"My head is pounding."

"Oh, let me get you some Tylenol and water. What about coffee? Do you want some coffee? Or wine? It's never too early. You know what, I will just go ahead and get it all for you."

Before I can respond, she is up and rushing to the kitchen.

"Yes to all of that, please," I say, making myself comfortable in the corner of the couch.

She quickly returns and hands me all the necessities. God bless moms.

"*So,* were you able to sleep at all? Have you heard from him?" No wasting time.

"Eh, kind of. And no, nothing."

"Wait, really? You haven't heard from him? Seriously?" She joins me on the couch. "After he let you drive to the airport by yourself? Not to mention completely distraught, and what... Just nothing?"

"No, but he must be doing just fine."

"Why do you say that? I don't think he is. He is probably just torn apart like you are."

"No, he isn't. Before Nate came over, I woke up to a text. A text from our premarital counselor saying how sorry she was."

This is so humiliating. I shouldn't have said anything.

"Wait, what?"

"Yup. Mom, it hasn't even been twenty-four hours and—and... He is already telling people." I'm biting my lip. *Hold it together, Alice.*

"What? Shut up. Okay, he has some nerve. How could he tell people without checking on you first?"

"Because he is done. I told you this last night. There is no discussion, no going back."

"Okay," she says, trying to calm herself as she rearranges books on the coffee table and puts a coaster under my mug. "Well, what about his family or friends? Have you heard from any of them?"

"Nope."

"Unbelievable," she takes a deep breath. "Okay, well, how can I help? What needs to get done?"

"It's fine. You have done enough already. I'll contact all the vendors and take care—"

"Alice, no. He should help you with that. He ended it, so he can go and clean up this mess."

"Mom, I'm the bride, and you know how that works out. I do all the planning and communication. He probably can't even tell you the name of our wedding coordinator. Or where the decorations were purchased from. It's easier if I do it."

"Alice, why are you making this easier for him? Do you not see this situation right now for what it is? He is such a—"

"Mom, please, I don't want to get into this right now. It's the last bit of control I feel I have between him and I."

She pauses and continues to rearrange books on the table. "I'm sorry, it's just that—"

"I know."

"Look, I know you don't want to talk, but your siblings have all asked if they can come home to see you. I told them I would check with you first, but you know them. They're all persistent."

Deep breath. A part of me wants to hide away in my room and never talk to or see a single person. However, I haven't seen my family in months, and having them here could be a good distraction.

"Sure," I say, "But can you please tell them I don't want too many questions about what happened. If they are going to come, I want it to be normal."

"I will let them know. And Alice, when you're ready to talk—"

"I know, Mom. Thank you."

I wish I could give my mom more right now. Answer more questions, show more gratitude, accept her help, but I can't. Even with the support system of my family and friends, I should feel like the most cared for girl in the world. But I don't. All of these people were getting ready to come watch me get married, and now they're seeing me as the girl left at the altar.

I couldn't be what David wanted, and now I'm letting down my family. What other disappointments will result from this breakup? My job? My future? My faith?

Even though David's decision is what put me here, my heart breaks for him. I imagine him back in Colorado, all alone, away from family. It takes everything in me not to reach out.

I pick up my phone and open up our text messages. The last few texts send a knife to my stomach.

David: *Haha, that gif always makes me laugh. Good one, babe.*

Wish you were here to distract me from work. Come home already.

You also looked so good leaving the house. Don't let those men at work check you out.

Once again, I'm left alone in the dark. Lost, confused, and longing to understand the mind of the man who held our future. The man who still, and may forever, have my heart.

*

I'm sitting on the couch when I hear the first of my family arrive. Usually, I would jump up from my seat and greet them before they reached the kitchen, but today I can't seem to get myself to even turn around.

One by one, nephews and nieces start filing inside, charging ahead as their parents try to keep up. I will admit, while not feeling my best, hearing their excitement to be at Grandma and Grandpa's brings me some joy.

The first face I see is my older sister, JA. She walks in, glowing and happy as always, which is her regardless of any situation at hand. Her positivity always radiates in every room she enters. But the moment our eyes meet, she skips past the usual hello's and joins me on the couch. Her arms squeeze tightly around me and catches my head on her shoulder, accepting and allowing my immediate loss of emotional control.

Welp. Putting on a brave face lasted about .02 seconds.

"Alice," is all she can get out as I let my tears fall.

It's all she needs to say to send me spiraling further. I can't imagine how uncomfortable this is for everyone to witness. I hate this.

"Why is Auntie Alice cwying?" I hear my niece ask out loud, joining us on the couch. "Auntie Alice, look at my new shoes! Aren't they pretty? And they're pink! I love pink. It's my *favewet* color."

The inability to annunciate her r's makes me laugh a little and catch my breath.

"Why are you cwying?"

"Auntie Alice is just a little sad," JA jumps in like an absolute mom. "Can you help Daddy bring things in from the car?"

This innocent interruption brings me back to center and gives an opportunity for everyone else to come up and give me a hug. It feels as if they are all lined up, ready to give their condolences.

You did this, David. You caused this, and I wish you cared. This is all I think as I throw on a pitiful smile for each awkward greeting.

Each embrace feels like a push toward having to face the reality of what happened. The more it settles, the more my body crumbles. My brother William walks in with dinner for everyone. The smell of food still makes me sick. I could hardly get coffee down this morning. No way is a taco going to be easy.

Everyone is doing their best to keep things feeling normal, talking about the stock market and weather with the local news playing in the background. Anything to help ease the awkwardness of the large elephant in the room. A part of me wishes I could be hiding underneath my bed sheets, but at least I can hide in a crowd of twelve people crammed in a kitchen.

I can't help but feel like the black sheep right now. No one has asked me about it yet. And I don't blame them. Who wants to be the first to ask? They already saw me lose control with JA. No one wants to be responsible for causing tears, but the thing is, they aren't the ones responsible for this. This is David's doing, and mine, I guess. I'm the one who failed to keep him.

Buzz buzz.

My phone vibrates on the counter, and my stomach drops even further when I see Erin's name pop up.

My hands get shaky, and my body language must signal SOS to my sister.

"Who is it? You okay?" She walks away from my niece, who is negotiating how many bites she had to eat until earning dessert.

"Yes, um, it's just—"

"David?" Mom quickly chimes in.

"No, not David. It's his mom."

"What did she say?" my mom and sister say simultaneously. The room slowly gets quiet. No one wants to miss what I am about to share.

"I—I don't know. I'm afraid to open it. I haven't even heard from David. I don't know if I am ready to hear from his mom..."

"Wait, you haven't heard from David?" Nate asks.

"At all?" Mitchell finishes Nate's thoughts.

So many brothers. So much unwanted attention right now. You can tell the tone of their voice is more protective and angry than it is empathetic. I can hear the guys continue to talk, and it's not anything good.

"Well, open it when you're ready," says my sister-in-law, Sarah, but the silence of the room gives me the impression that they are anxious to know what is happening. So I open my phone.

Erin: *Alice, I am so sorry. I just got off the phone with David and heard the news. Praying for you. Let me know if there is anything I can do to help. I just don't have any words. I'm so sorry.*

"Is it bad? Are you okay to share it?" JA asks.

I hand my phone to her and let her read it and share with the room. My throat is choked as I do my best to hold in the overwhelming flood of tears.

Hold it together, Alice.

The room is quiet, listening to every little word. I want to run—anything to escape this embarrassment.

"Wait a minute, he *just* told his parents?" my mom clarifies. "Wasn't he *just* home with his parents last week? He didn't share anything with them? And didn't you say he was already telling other people?"

Her question opens the flood gate. Silence now feels damn near impossible at this point as everyone starts to speak up.

"What is this guy's problem?"

"Who doesn't tell his parents right away?"

"What is wrong with him?"

"I want to fly out to Colorado right now and give him a piece of mind. He can't do this to my daughter."

"I always knew something was off about him."

"How could he do this to Alice? Of all people... Alice?"

The comments and words used to describe him get increasingly worse. My family is protective, and the anger is understandable, but I love him. I don't know what to say or how to make it all stop. My sanity needs a minute, or one hundred, so I head to the nearest bedroom and let myself crash on the mattress.

Knock knock.

I knew it wouldn't take too long before someone followed me in here.

"Hey, it's me," JA makes her way on the bed with me. "Alice, I'll just go ahead and say it. One day you will look back and be so thankful you didn't marry him. You deserve better than this."

How? I love him. He was who I chose for life. He was everything I wanted.

"And I know how much you loved him," she continues through my silence and tears. "You sacrificed *a lot* to be with him. More so than he did for you. And honestly, I don't think he ever truly appreciated that from you."

"No, I think he sacrificed too—"

"Alice, you left your life behind in California for this guy. All of your family, friendships, and belongings. You had to find a new job, deal with crazy new roommates, crazy cold weather, and snowstorms. I only say all of this because you did a lot for him, and what he is doing to you right now is inexcusable."

"Well, none of that matters anymore. He doesn't care."

"This is hard to hear, Alice, even harder to say it, but I don't think he ever cared for you the way you cared for him."

"What? No, he was so amazing and loved me."

"Alice, look where you are at. This is not love. Regardless of his reason for ending it, the way he has dropped you out of his life is so far from love. Seeing you like this breaks my heart."

"But he did. I know he did. I thought he did. I mean, during the morning of the breakup and the weeks leading up to it, nothing in his behavior pointed to this. Even the day before our breakup, he left me a random sticky note with '*I love you*' written on it."

"Well, I can't explain his behavior and certainly don't understand it, but you're going to be so much better off without him. I know it."

There is a moment of silence between us. JA has always been a role model in my life, someone I know I can trust and who will tell things to me straight when I need to hear it. This may not be what I want to hear or remotely close to how I feel toward David right now, but a small part of me still trusts her words.

I grab my phone and open up the text from David's mom to reply.

Me: *Thank you for reaching out. I don't have many words right now. I'm home right now with family. They are taking good care of me.*

"How does that sound?" showing the phone to JA.

"Perfect."

Pressing send, I leave it at that and don't expect a response. At this point, I need to let go of any and all expectations. I have had enough letdowns.

Chapter Four

———

The weekend was bittersweet. On the one hand, it was amazing to be surrounded by family, but on the other, I felt a sense of relief once everyone left. It's draining to keep a smile on my face while trying not to lose it every time someone asks how I'm feeling. Everyone was well-intentioned, but the questions were endless. *"Are you leaving Colorado? Do you have to quit your job? Do you need help calling wedding vendors? Have you told other guests yet? Are you moving home? Have you heard from him yet?"* Questions that I hadn't even begun to think about.

Stay in Colorado? I can't even begin to fathom what that would feel like. David was my only reason for moving there. And now I don't have him, or any relationship for that matter. Just the thought of running into him gives me anxiety. We built a life there. There is more to sacrifice and divide beyond our belongings.

Who would give up going to the market on Wednesday evenings? Who wouldn't hike our favorite trail ever again? Who would switch churches? Who would quit the gym first? Who gets to claim our favorite restaurant? Do we divide up the friends we've made there too? Every single aspect of our lives was intertwined. Every memory I have of that state, every inch of that city I touched, holds him in it.

My family is right, though. I do have to find a way to get my stuff out of his place, which isn't too much. We did sell and donate a lot of my belongings. He even helped me drop things off at Goodwill and reminded me to "keep the receipt for tax write-offs."

Did he know then that he was going to end our relationship? The least he could have done was tell me to hold onto a few basic things for the day I would wind up single.

It's almost been a week, and still no word from him. Every time my phone goes off, I hope to see his name. But it's never his. However, it appears word is traveling fast. Each day brings a new set of people who hear the news and send me their "*love*" and "*prayers*." Texts start to all sound the same: well-intentioned, but not the people I want to hear from.

I want to hear from David.

*

My body is weak and frail. I finally made an effort to get out for fresh air today. It took me thirty-five minutes to complete a mile. I can't believe how much of a physical toll this has taken on my body. It was only a matter of days ago where I was on a strict diet and workout plan for the wedding, averaging four miles of running a day to get my body prepped for the wedding. Now I can barely make it through a simple walk.

As I brush my teeth and get ready for the workday, I take notice of how puffy my eyes are from last night. Thank goodness my company has allowed me to work from home while I figure out this mess. And they don't have to see me so distressed after a rough night.

It wouldn't have been such a rough night, except I discovered David had taken down our wedding website. For the first time, I actually crawled into bed without feeling like I was ready to cry myself to sleep. Instead, I felt a tug to reread our "love story," but I should have known better. Nothing good would come from visiting the page and reminiscing on our special story. However, that feeling didn't matter because as soon as I went searching for the page, it was nowhere to be found.

The audacity, David.

I couldn't believe it. In fact, I refused to believe it. So I texted my best friend, Dev, and made her look it up. No luck. Once again, another executive decision was made on my behalf. Dev's response was, "That jerk just doesn't quit, huh? Must be nice not to have any emotions or care for others."

In a way, Dev is right. David hasn't cared to check in with me, and he had no problem taking down our wedding website. No one ever checks those things anyways, so why delete it so fast? Is he trying to reinforce his power? What is he trying to prove? I'm already left with nothing in my childhood home. Is that not enough shame to deal with?

The annoying part is that *I* was the one who put so much work into making the website. *I* uploaded everyone's emails into our spreadsheets. *I* wrote our love story. *I* designed every inch. And without notice—poof! It's gone.

*

Four o'clock rolls around, and I join my mom on the couch for another HGTV episode. The day was fairly productive. I had tackled some of the new projects I was given after receiving my promotion. There isn't a shortage of work, and it's a helpful distraction. Although, something tells me I won't be able to hold onto this promotion if I don't stay in Colorado. From endless emails and calls to *"check-in"* or responses such as *"we can review once you're back in the office,"* it is clear that my presence in the office is pertinent to the success of this role.

"Where is today's house flip taking place?" I ask my mom. We have watched so much HGTV I'm confident I could flip any house for millions.

"Small town in Tennessee. Look at all that land. Isn't it beautiful there?"

"Yes, it's so green. I wish my company had an office there; I would relocate in a heartbeat."

"Are you done with work for the day?"

"Yeah, my brain is fried at this point. Plus, everyone is in a later time zone, and they're out of the office by this point for a company Happy Hour. Must be nice."

"I'm sorry, but hey, I have to run to the market to grab some items for dinner tonight. Do you want to come?" my mom asks. She has been trying to get me out of the house.

"Eh, I don't know. I think I am okay."

"Come on. It'll be nice to go for a drive and get out a bit. Plus, I thought we could pick out some snacks to take for our weekend to Santa Barbara."

"Santa Barbara?"

"Yes, I know how much you love it there, and JA invited us to come. I already told her yes. It'll be good for you, good for us, to have fresh beach air."

Another well-intentioned gesture, but do they not understand how exhausted I am from last weekend? Now I have to do that all over again? Although, my mom is right. I do love Santa Barbara. The perfect weather makes it relaxing.

However, this is also the place where David told me he loved me. It holds such a different meaning to me now. Now I'm torn. I don't want to let my family down or for them to think I don't appreciate their efforts to cheer me up. Maybe going to the store with my mom right now is practice for getting back out there and socializing again.

"Okay, fine. But next time, ask me before signing me up for something."

"So that's a yes to the market?"

"Yes."

"Great, we will leave in twenty minutes. I can't wait," she cries, celebrating her victory in convincing me to get out of the house.

Porterville is a small town. My childhood was wonderful, but I wouldn't ever consider moving back permanently. You can't go anywhere without running into someone. Hence the stress I feel as I stare at my messy suitcases before me. *What do I wear?*

After four outfit changes, a few power stances in the mirror, and lots of concealer to help my puffy eyes, I land on a floral, flowy dress and pair it with sneakers. Dressed up yet casual. If I'm going to face hardships, I'm going to do it in style. Nothing screams "*I got this under control*" like a well-dressed woman.

"Almost ready?" my mom yells out. She probably wasn't expecting me to get this ready for a trip to the store.

I throw on a little more makeup to cover my red cheeks and the bags that have set up camp underneath my eyes. I take one last deep breath as I look in the mirror.

Here goes nothing.

*

"Do you think people know?" I ask my mom on our drive.

"What? How would people know?"

"People talk, ya know? I don't know. Maybe it's just my paranoia. I also deleted photos off my Instagram of him and I. Plus, my wedding that was supposed to happen a few days ago didn't happen, so…"

"Alice, I think you are giving social media too much of your energy. I doubt anyone knows."

I hope she's right.

As we get closer to the store, I feel knots tightening in my stomach. What's odd about this feeling is that I don't even know who I fear seeing the most. Regardless, I can't help but feel that no matter how much makeup I put on or what dress I wear, there is a sign across my forehead that says "failed engagement."

We grab our cart and make our way through the store. First in the cart is wine to pair with a simple charcuterie board, which has become our staple snack for our many evenings on the couch. I'm setting the box of crackers in the cart when suddenly I hear a familiar voice.

"Carla! Alice! Hi!"

"Hi, Christine," my mom says to her, and I stop in my tracks. Here we go. First the airport with Holli and now here? Can't I ever catch a break?

Christine is a dear family friend, and I grew up closely with her daughters. We played sports together, went to school together, and vacationed together. She is wonderful, but I know this conversation is going to head in a direction I was hoping to avoid.

"Oh my goodness, so good to see you both! Gosh, it's been so long," Christine reaches out for a hug, "And oh my goodness, Alice! You're in town, what are you doing here? Are you still living in Colorado?"

So many questions. Valid questions. But so many questions.

"No, well yes, I'm just home for a bit right now," I say, keeping it as vague as possible. I can feel my mom's eyes on me, watching me closely.

"Oh, how fun! And aren't you getting married soon? Or did you already get married? I can't seem to keep up. There's so much going on these days, and you kids all grow up so fast!"

My body is tensing up, and I can see my mom is trying to decide if she should jump in on my behalf.

"Actually, um..." doing my best to get through this somewhat poised. "Actually... I'm—I'm not getting married."

"Oh no," Christine's shoulders drop. "Alice, why? What happened?"

Deep breath again. I'm biting my lip as my mom puts her arm around me.

"Well, no, my fiancé, David, or ex, I should say. I don't really know what to call him anymore. He, um... He—"

"He called it off," my mom comes in for the rescue. "It was horrible, Christine. Out of the blue ended everything with her. We are so devastated but so thankful we have Alice here to take care of her during this time."

"Oh my goodness, Alice, I—I had no idea. I'm so sorry. I wouldn't have asked if I knew."

"No, no, it's okay, you didn't know," I say, gently wiping my eyes and forcing a smile.

"I'm sorry, I don't know what to say. But you look great, and I'm happy you're home."

"It's okay. Thank you."

"I swear just the other day, the girls and I were talking about how we couldn't wait to see you postwedding pictures, and now... I mean, wow, I'm so sorry. Come here, let me give you another hug."

This look. This tone. This response. It's becoming all too familiar when I break the news to people. I should be celebrating this week and a new chapter in my life as a wife, not grieving the loss of it.

Running into old friends in your hometown shouldn't look like crying next to the rotisserie chickens. But I remind myself that I put on the dress and made a choice to come out in public. I refuse to let this conversation end on a sad note, so before we part ways, I ask about one of her daughters, who is currently engaged and planning a wedding.

To my surprise, this isn't hard to ask and actually makes me feel a little better on the inside. My anger and disappointment aren't toward others; they're toward David.

Christine shares all the details and updates about her daughter's upcoming wedding, but all I can think about is David.

The man is not very social. He is probably alone in his apartment right now in Colorado, keeping to himself. When he goes to the store, he won't run into anyone because he doesn't have many people to run into there. David doesn't have to get dressed up to prove to those around him that he is okay or show he will survive this crisis and come out stronger.

It pains me to come to this realization, but his life is probably still fairly normal.

As soon as we get back in the car, my mom speaks up. "Alice, I'm so proud of you. I know that had to be hard."

"Yes, it was, but what can you do?"

"And that was kind of you to ask about the upcoming wedding too... Was it hard for you to hear about someone else's wedding? I was surprised you even asked."

"Actually, no. I'm happy for Christine and her daughter. They weren't the ones who hurt me. David did. Plus, I'd rather talk about their wedding than my failed one anyways."

The drive home is quiet, and I decide it's time I reach out to David. Clearly, he isn't going to make an effort to contact me. It's time for me to take matters into my own hands and start my path of moving forward.

Chapter Five

After dinner, I join my parents in the family room to watch Jeopardy, a game I'm horrible at. The only question I answer correctly is, *"This movie starred the actress, Reese Wither-spoon, and took place at Harvard."* Too easy. *Legally Blonde,* duh. And what girl isn't empowered by Elle Woods in *Legally Blonde* to go out there and stick it to a guy who failed to see the value and worth in a woman. I love it. Reminds me I need to rewatch it.

I find my cozy spot on the couch beside my parents and scroll aimlessly through my phone, working up the courage to reach out to David. One part of me wants to run it by my parents or Dev. Another part of me feels like I should have every right to reach out to David. He was my fiancé only a week ago. So why do I feel like a bother? If I ask others for opinions, it will turn into a bigger discussion, and I don't need the opinions of others. What I need is to channel my inner Elle Woods and be strong, direct, and assertive.

Closing out of Instagram, I pull up David's name in my text messages and start typing. Wait, should I call him instead? Catch him off guard? It's only fair for him to receive what he gave me.

But what if I call and he doesn't answer? Another rejection.

What if I call and I can't hold myself together? Another embarrassment.

What if I call and he doesn't sound upset or bothered? Another disappointment.

What if I call and he is with others, or another girl? Another unforeseen curveball.

"What are you doing over there?" My mom interrupted my thoughts.

"Nothing, just scrolling," I lie, but for a good reason. This needs to be between me and David.

All right. I bring my focus back to the phone. I can't call him. I wish I could listen to his voice one last time, but I can't. The other night I listened to old voicemails from him because I missed the sound of his voice. However, if I want to remain strong in front of him, unlike I did when he broke up with me, then I need to stick to texting for now. Otherwise, I will fold. He still has this unexplainable power over me. Crazy to think how fast we went from talking all day every day to being terrified to dial his number.

Here we go.

Me: *Hey, I need to figure out dates and times to come out and gather my stuff from your apartment. I was thinking about coming in about two weeks when flight tickets are more manageable, taking into consideration that my parents have to come to help me pack as well. Would that work for you?*

Quick reread and send. Straight to the point. With a jab of letting him know that I now have to drag my parents into this mess, and yes, it's going to cost us more booking flights and a hotel. I already had to dismiss my parent's question about how much my last-minute flight *really* was. Let's just say booking a few hours before for a one-way ticket to California is not cheap.

Five minutes pass and my nerves are heightened, but I'm trying to stay calm, so my mom doesn't suspect anything again.

Buzz buzz.

David: **Yup, that works. Would that Saturday from eleven to three give you enough time?**

Four hours. My eyes shutter as I reread the text because this has to be a joke. Four hours? Four freaking hours to sort through everything and pack up my whole life? Not to mention deal with all the wedding gifts to separate what is mine from his in the garage.

Also, what is up with this message? So businesslike and cold. All right, yes, my message wasn't decorated with rose petals and rainbows, but c'mon. David hurt me. He made this decision. How can he no longer care? No "nice to hear from you," or "how are you doing since I ruined your life?"

Screw the tears this time. My blood is boiling.

Me: **Four hours is not sufficient, nor do I want to be constrained. That is my whole life I need to pack up. I think a Friday and Saturday option would be nice. It's the least you can do, David...**

Send. I look at the red heart emoji next to his name as I reread my message. This needs to be removed as soon as possible. But how did we get to this place of being so cold, so distant? And why am I negotiating time to gather my belongings? How can he view this as a negotiable topic? This is my life we're talking about.

Buzz buzz.

David: **Okay, fine. I guess that works. Just confirm once flights are booked, and you are actually coming.**

Me: **Okay. Also, I can sort through the wedding gifts and figure those out.**

David: *Thumbs up*

Thumbs up? Wow. I wait a few minutes and see if he starts to type again. Surely deep down he wants to ask how I'm doing, right? But as I stare at the screen, the disappointment increases because nothing points to him typing again. He's done with the conversation.

Why does he get to be the one to decide it ends? He can't continue to get away with this behavior without knowing how it's making me feel. Maybe I let this slide during our relationship, but that relationship no longer exists, and he is now going to hear how I'm really feeling.

Me: *And David, while we're here. Do you mind stopping the wedding un-planning? I was the one who did just about everything, so I can handle it. Or at least run it by me before you go off and make another rash decision or tell random people. It would have been nice to send communication out from the both of us. It's been so choppy and embarrassing coming from both ends. I don't know if you remember, but it was our wedding, not yours.*

David: *I was just trying to help so you wouldn't have to worry about it.*

My fingers fire away without giving any thought or consideration to my message before hitting send.

Me: *David, you aren't worried about me. You're only worried about yourself. If you actually cared, you would have checked in on me.*

David: *Alice, just let me know the dates and times. Bye.*

He completely avoided the call-out of my last message.

Okay, maybe I shouldn't have taken the first opportunity to shoot jabs at him, but c'mon. I'm clearly the lowest priority for him now. When did that happen? And how did it happen so fast? I should be the one making him work, yet once again, I'm over here unable to evoke any inkling of emotion out of him.

Is this how it always was?

I open up my phone again and find flights for us to travel back to Colorado. Dev also already agreed to come out and help, so I will have her join later in the week. Each of them said they would be ready to go at a moment's notice, so I don't draw attention to it and book whatever has the most appealing price on those dates. Between old flight credit and reward points I racked up, the cost is somewhat bearable. Book and buy. Let's get this over with.

"All right, I am heading off to bed," I say.

"Already? It's so early? Everything okay?" my dad asks.

"Yeah, I'm pretty tired. Also, flights to Colorado are booked. I forwarded the confirmation to you both," I say, continuing forward before I'm bogged with any more questions.

"Wait," my mom mutes the TV. "Did you confirm this with David? Does he know we're coming?"

"Yes, he knows."

"Oh! So he finally reached out to you?" my mom asks.

My dad finishes her thought. "Well, it's about time. I hope he offered to pay for the flights too."

"No, he didn't reach out. I did." Admitting this kills me. I hate being the one who caved and reached out first. "And no, he didn't offer to buy the tickets. He won't either. At this point, I wouldn't expect anything from him."

"What is his deal?" my dad fires off. "Does he think he is freed from all this trouble he caused you?"

"Yeah, why does he think he gets to act this way?" my mom continues.

"I know, I know. Trust me, I'm just as lost as you two, but I don't want to get into this. I'm going to go to bed. I love you guys and thank you for being willing to join me on the second-worst flight of my life," I sarcastically follow this with a smile and head for the bathroom to start my nighttime routine.

From the bathroom, I hear my parents continue to talk. They're exchanging theories on David and why he is doing this and why he ended our engagement. It's wasted time, though. There is no point in trying to understand him. At least my parents and I are in the boat together. Paddling in what feels like never-ending circles, unsure where the shore is and when this storm ends.

*

The weekend could not have come sooner. The drive to Santa Barbara is about three and half hours, so I make myself cozy in the backseat letting Nate and my parents lead conversations and music selections. Normally I love car rides because you get everyone's undivided attention, but today I'm not in the mood for chatting. I'm ready to feel the coastal breeze and hopefully relax. I do feel somewhat less stressed now that I have my flights booked for Colorado.

Ping ping.

New email notification

We aren't even two hours into the drive. I should ignore this, but in the preview, I see David's name.

Why is he emailing me?

Something about the subject line makes me nervous about opening it, but I'm anxious to know.

From: David

Subject line: Change of plans

My heart is racing, and my palms are sweaty. What does "change of plans" mean? Oh my gosh, what if this is an email he sent to everyone regarding a change of plans for our wedding? Or maybe it's for a vendor, and he included me? At this point, I can't predict his actions, but seeing his name in my email hits hard. I'm doing everything I can to keep myself together to avoid any suspicion in the car.

David and I used to always email for fun. Felt a little old school versus the day-to-day texting. He would send me funny videos, future homes he thought I would like, or dream vacations we should go on some day, but I know this email won't be any of those. If it was anything like his texting the other day, it's going to send me spiraling again. Last night I sent him a text confirming the dates and time I would be in Colorado, per his request, but he never responded. So what the heck could this be about? Before I could talk myself out of it, I opened the email.

Alice, I received your confirmation of your travel dates and time for when you will be here. Thank you.

I have given it some thought, and I am not comfortable with you being in my apartment when I am not there, but I would still like to honor your plans of coming out during the dates you selected. With that said, I have gone ahead and packed up your stuff and placed everything into a storage unit. I made sure it was nicely packed and stored. I also included wedding gifts that were from your side of the guest list. You can choose to do with these however you wish, but I would recommend returning them.

The key to the storage unit, along with additional information, is on its way to your parent's house, and here is the tracking number. The storage unit is paid for until the end of the month.

Attached is the location of the storage unit and a drawn-out map that will show which unit contains your belongings.
   Best,

"Oh my god," I say out loud as my tears start to fall. I'm once again at a complete loss for words.

Nate is on the phone with a friend, and I suddenly hear him say, "Hey dude, I have to go." Exactly the kind of attention I didn't want while being trapped in a car for several hours. No room to escape to when I want to hide my feelings.

"Alice, are you okay?" Nate asks. "What happened? Is it David?"

My parents have now turned down the radio and directed their attention to me, asking the same questions. I can't get myself to find words, so I hand my phone to Nate with the email open and listen as he reads it out loud.

"Wait, he just put your stuff in a storage unit?" my mom clarifies.

"Yeah, what the actual fuck is his problem, Alice?" Nate's voice is raised. David woke the bear. "Why is he treating you this way? I don't care what happened between you two. I wouldn't even care if you were the one who ended it, but this is just disrespectful."

I'm trying to listen to them, but I actually think I might throw up.

"Dad, pull over," I say.

"What? Why?" he asks.

"Dad, I need to throw up. Pull over!"

My dad pulls into the emergency lane along one of California's busiest highways, and I stumble out of the car, lean my body over, and throw up. Hundreds of cars pass. People probably assume I'm car sick. They wouldn't for a moment think I'm sick from pain caused by one man. My mom jumps out and grabs my hair to put it up in a bun. Meanwhile, my dad is offering me water.

"Alice, I'm so sorry," my dad says as I raise my head and take the water bottle from his hand. "But he can't do this. He can't just go and move your belongings without your permission. That's not okay."

"It's not okay. I hate this, Dad. So much." I pinch my eyes, ashamed. "But I can't do anything. I left the state. I left my stuff behind in *his* apartment. There isn't anything I can do to change him or change his mind. Trust me. I wish I could."

Tears turn to sobs, and I can barely get the water down.

My family continues on, questioning everything. Everyone is feeling a little lost. This behavior is so unlike him. We saw David as a man of integrity who held himself and others to high standards. Between the three of them, they are starting to tear him apart, and this is exactly why I can't allow myself to crumble in front of others. I understand I am hurt, but they are also turning on him faster than I thought. Are these deeper opinions of theirs I failed to see or listen to in the past? Or is it strictly a response from everything he is doing to me?

My heart is worn.

After about ten minutes, my stomach feels settled enough to get back into the car. I ask everyone if we can keep me getting sick between us. I don't need more people worried or asking questions. For the duration of the ride, I put my headphones in and leaned my head on the window.

Ping ping.

Dev responds to the screenshot of the email: ***No, absolutely not. This is a joke, right? The audacity! Alice, please let me text him and give him a piece of mind. He just packed up everything of yours? Your intimates? Dirty laundry?***

What about your wedding dress? Everything? Yet he can't talk to you like a proper human? What is his deal? I feel horrible not being there with you. How can I help? What can I do?

She is spot on, saying what I still don't have the courage to say about David, but I don't have the energy to respond.

With David, I thought I had found my great love. He was the kind of man who wanted to protect me, keep me from anything harmful. He was always teaching me new things and showing me new ways to think about situations. David was the person who would make sure I recovered from workouts properly, kept me away from unhealthy habits, helped me to stop texting and driving, and taught me to become more mindful of content I consumed (such as binging a season of The Real Housewives on the weekend). He didn't like it if a coworker treated me poorly or if he felt a male coworker was too friendly. He took notice and protected me. At least I thought it was protection, but maybe it was just control? Either way, I was David's girl. People knew that. But maybe that's all I was to him, some sort of property. Something he owned.

That's the unfortunate truth about property. It can be thrown out easily or even one day stored away in a storage unit.

I know I have to respond. I have to stand up for myself.

At first, I type out a very lengthy, emotional response to his email, listing out every little action he has done to hurt me, but I decide not to send it. It's clear now I can't get through to him. What's the point even trying?

Instead, I respond, *"This is not what we agreed to, and I am not okay with it. I expected more from you, David."*

Nothing I can ever say or do will change his mind or his behavior. This is how it's going to be moving forward, but maybe this is how it's always been? I failed to see it because I was on his side of the story. David was king. He ruled, and I followed, until one day, I stopped following. Is that when he realized his power was going to be challenged?

Dreamers are like that. They put on rose-colored glasses and ignore reality. Then those glasses get ripped off somehow, and they can't stand the violent blues stabbing their eyes and turn away.

Chapter Six

———

Sounds of children screaming and the smell of barbecue fill the backyard. The weather in Santa Barbara could not be more perfect. The breeze is light, the sun is shining, and the temperature is perfect for a good sweater-with-shorts combination. My family and I are in the backyard enjoying drinks while the kids run around. It's a nice distraction from the incident on the way here.

"Hey, Alice," my brother-in-law, Robert, turns from the grill. "So, you know that small race I'm running tomorrow?"

"The half marathon?" I clarify.

"Yes. Well, our trainer said we are welcome to bring along anyone to join, and I was thinking, if you're up for it, you should join us too."

Completely caught off guard, I raise one eyebrow and shoot him a *"you are crazy"* look, paired nicely with a chuckle, thinking this has to be a joke. No way am I in a position to run a half marathon. Yes, a week ago, I was training hard for the wedding, but I've also hardly eaten, slept, or gone more than three hours without crying. Not to mention the fiasco I just had on the side of a highway. This is the worst idea.

"Um, no way. Probably not a good idea for me."

"C'mon, I really think you could crush it. You've always been a good runner, and the group is so welcoming. There isn't pressure to go fast or set a personal record. It's truly just running for completion."

"Just racing for completion? What kind of race is that?" my dad jokingly chimes in.

"That's the thing. The run is a half marathon, from pier to peak, meaning you gain a little over four thousand feet in elevation. So essentially, it's a thirteen-mile climb." Robert pauses, realizing what he just divulged because that sounds absolutely insane. "But Alice, I'm telling you, you can do it. Plus, the view at the top is worth it. You will finish above the clouds."

"Oh, I don't know. If it were any other time, maybe, but I don't think I am in a position to take on this kind of course."

"Alice, I think you are underestimating yourself," my dad chips in. "You can do it. You have always been this kind of athlete who can jump in and do anything. I'll even help drive along the way and bring you water too."

"Dad, what? No. Thank you, but no, there is no way."

"Just give it some thought. We do have to wake up at 4 a.m., so you do need to decide fast, but listen to me, listen to your dad. You can do it." Robert finishes as he puts the grilled chicken on a plate and heads back inside.

Everyone is inside, getting plates ready and seating the kids. While my dad and I wait outside, he turns to me and says, "Alice, you should run tomorrow." I sit there not only debating if I'm going to run or not but whether or not I even want to eat tonight. Does he not realize I'm still recovering from the incident earlier in the car?

"Dad, why are you so persistent on this? You saw me earlier; my body is not equipped for a run, let alone a race at *that* level of difficulty."

"Alice, you are stronger than you think. I know you. It's mind over matter. I saw you overcome challenges as an athlete growing up, and I think this is another one for you to take on. Claim back that strength within you."

My dad doesn't get emotional. This broken engagement hasn't just shattered my heart, but my family's. Dad especially. He didn't ask to watch his daughter go through this trauma. So when I open my mouth, I can't believe the words that come out.

"Okay, fine, I will do it. But you have to promise you'll be there when I finish... Or if I don't finish. I don't want to pass out going up that mountain."

"Alice, you won't pass out, but I'll be there. You can count on that."

Robert peeks his head back out the door. "So, is that a yes?"

"Heck yeah, Alice is coming back," my dad cheers.

*

Why did I agree to run this race?

I could throw my phone across the room. The alarm is way too loud for 3:30 a.m. As if my sleep hasn't suffered enough this past week, it was definitely a mess last night from the stress of this run mixed with David's email.

My professional running attire isn't here, so I make do with what I have: comfort, reliability, and a really tight sports bra to hold the babies up. Luck is on my side for once. Most everything is in Colorado, and the majority of what I brought is for walking on the beach. But I've got enough gear to make this work.

"How are you feeling? Ready? I am so pumped you agreed to do this with me," Robert greets me as I head into the kitchen for a quick cup of coffee.

"Honestly, I just need to get there and start running before my body realizes what I am actually doing," I joke with him. "I am telling you now that I hope everyone is ready to wait for me at the top of the mountain. This is going to be brutal."

"No way, you got this. I wouldn't invite you if I didn't think you had it in you," Robert says. "I'm ready to head out when you are."

*

The first three miles are in complete darkness since we started before sunrise. Not the safest start to a race, but between our camera flashlights and empty streets, we're able to make our way. I stay with Rob, or I should say he stays with me, and we start off slow and steady, knowing that a thirteen-mile climb is not something you can sprint.

Mile four is our first rest stop and the beginning of the sun is starting to peak out. My dad already headed further up the mountain after I told him there was already a rest station set up at this point.

"How are you feeling?" Robert asks.

"Honestly, I feel great."

"Well, hey, don't let me stop you. I'm going to wait until the rest of the group gets here, but if you want to take off, go for it," Robert's encouragement is freeing. Maybe it's still too early for my brain to fully understand what I am doing, or maybe it's the endorphins kicking in, but I'm ready to take off on my own.

"All right, I'll take you up on that. See you at the top!" I shout back as I head forward.

Alone now, I plug in my earbuds and start playing an old Spotify playlist I created for a half marathon I ran about two years ago. This sends me back into a memory from Colorado. It was my first race since moving there, and I was so nervous about how the elevation would affect me. But I ran it to prove that I could acclimate to the new weather in the new state and show David that "his girl" was, in fact, an athlete.

When I signed up for the race, I dreamt about the finish line and running into David's arms. He would embrace me and not care for how sweaty or gross I might be, showing me that he was nothing but proud of what I had accomplished. However, David didn't go to that race. He went on a hunting trip instead. I also remember him not being too keen about me spending $150 to "just run thirteen miles," and that I could "go do that for free on any given day," and he could "watch me run another time."

However, I still crushed the race that day. Even without him there. I was so determined to do well and report back to him that his girl was strong. Or maybe I was just fearful of reporting that I didn't do well and the $150 was a waste? *Hmm.*

This playlist is straight fire, though. I love all my girly pop hits, mixed with some old-school hip hop that puts me in a competitive headspace. Looking down at my watch, I see another mile and a half have passed. I'm cruising without any notice, which is every runner's goal. Able to enjoy the scenery, own the adrenaline, and stay focused on the miles ahead.

Until this next song hits.

I forgot about this part of the playlist. Since David wasn't going to be there for my race, I asked him to give me a few songs that would remind me of him when they played. It was my personal way of including him in the race with me.

Do I let it play through or skip it?

EDM music was never my thing, and I only added it because of him. This song takes me back to the moment I crossed the finish line in my Colorado race. Exhausted and alone, I watched people around me get hugs and cheers from their people. But I put on a smile, told people it didn't bother me, and posted photos like it was the greatest day ever. Later that night, I got a text from David after his day of hunting to let me know he didn't catch a single animal. He was upset. We talked all about his hunting adventures that night. The only thing he really inquired about my run was whether or not I set a new personal record, called PR, and how I ranked in my age group.

How did I brush that behavior off? It's starting to make me sick of how much I wanted his approval.

Screw this. I'm changing songs.

Who was he to ask if I PR'd on the race? He didn't run it. I did. I should have reminded him he left me alone while I supported his new hobby and friends. My support never subsided, while his never existed.

Why was it so hard for him to acknowledge that he wasn't the only one in the relationship who could be successful?

These thoughts drive me up a wall. Before now, I wasn't fully aware of what pushed me deep down to agree to this race today, but now it's clear why I'm here. This run is not about proving to anyone else that I can do this, but rather proving to myself I have the vigor to push through hard things in life.

As the miles go on, I continue passing other members who started in earlier heats before our group. My dad was at mile six like he said he would be, and I barely stopped for a quick swig of water and electrolytes. Not needing much rest time, I took off quickly and told him to drive up to about mile nine. At first, he sounded concerned about leaving me alone as I headed up this mountain, but I reassured him I was doing just fine. It's a paved road without any other cars in sight. I've got this. I'm okay on my own.

Mile nine rolls up faster than I expect, and I hear my dad yell out, "Hey, need some more water?" from his car window.

"Oh my gosh, yes!" I cry, tossing him my empty water bottle.

"How are you feeling? You sure you don't need me to track alongside you?" he asks.

"Honestly, I feel good. I can't believe I'm already nine miles in; time just started to fly by."

"Yeah, you are cruising by everyone. You have at least a quarter to a half-mile on the next person behind you."

"What? No way..."

I can't believe I'm actually that far ahead of others.

"Yup! You go, girl. But do you need me to drive alongside you?" he asks again.

"Dad, I'm okay. I think being alone is good for me right now. I can do it. I'll see you around mile ten or eleven."

"Okay, well, call me if you need anything. I'm serious. This mountain is no joke."

With a smile and a wave, I watch him take off ahead. Glancing down at my watch again, I can't believe the pace I'm maintaining. Certainly, at some point, my body will give out. But until then, I'm going to keep pushing it.

Once I see my dad has fully turned the corner, I'm back to being with my own thoughts. Deep down, I don't want anger toward David to be what carries me up this mountain. But I also don't want it to be sadness or pity from others.

I think about David putting my stuff in a storage unit. I think about that receipt I saw on the counter as I packed my bags. I think about the moving papers. I think about his disregard for what I wanted, what I needed, and his lack of empathy.

Anger and resentment won't help me heal, or anything else for that matter. And I can't let him steal any more of my joy or spirit. It's at this moment where I decide to pray out loud. This is actually something I witnessed a family doing during a race back in San Francisco many years ago. It was so powerful that the memory stayed etched in my brain and inspired me to do the same. My surroundings are so serene and the quiet, calm morning gives a sense of peace that my prayers are safe, right here right now.

I start by listing out things I'm grateful for.

"God, thank you for my family. Their support and encouragement to get me through this past week and up this hill. Thank you for family and friends who continue to love me endlessly when others couldn't.

"Thank you for the beautiful morning. The perfect, calm sea breeze is keeping me cool and relaxed.

"Thank you for my job and being able to work from California.

"Thank you for Holli and her company on the flight.

"Thank you for giving my body the strength to be running right now.

"And this next one is hard but thank you for protecting me from what I failed to see. I don't know what it is you're keeping me from, God, but thank you."

As my perspective starts to shift, my eyes water. Amidst the hardest week of my life, I've also been shown how blessed my life is through the amount of support I've had.

"God help me trust what you have ahead.

"Give me the strength to come out of this stronger, wiser, and more sure of the woman I am.

Help me to trust one day again."

Barely able to get the rest of my thoughts out as my chest tightens.

"Help me... Help me have faith in love again. Let me turn this into something beautiful: a story that isn't wasted on tears but built on resilience."

And just when I think I might be ready to collapse, there is an urge in me to continue praying. This time it isn't to pray for myself, but instead for David.

"I don't know where David is right now or where he is headed, but I hope he is okay.

"Help him, Lord.

"Help his heart.

"Guide him.

"I wish I knew what he was going through. I would do anything to understand, but my biggest hope is that he isn't alone.

"I hope he leans on you for direction and healing in this time.

"I hope he knows how much I loved him, how much I still love him."

The words aren't grand, and I'm certainly not in a place to forgive, but it's a start. Even in times of resenting him for what he did, what he didn't do, and what his actions will cause in my future, my love for him still stands.

As I start to round another corner, I see my dad's car, which means I'm at mile ten or eleven, but when I look down at my watch, I'm surprised to see 12.15 miles.

"What? I am further along than I thought," I say to my dad when I reach the car, guzzling down the water he tosses out to me.

"Don't you want to break for a minute?" my dad asks as I start trekking forward.

"No, I'm good. Remember what you told me yesterday? I got this, Dad!"

"All right, all right. Well, I'm going to wait here until Rob comes through, and then I'll join you up there," he says to me. "Go claim that mountain."

And with those words, I am fueled for the finish line. I look up at the remainder of this climb. It really is straight up hill. No give or breaks. The weather could not be more perfect, though. The sun is slowly peeking through the trees, just enough to give brightness but not enough to burden you with the heat.

Finish line this way.

Finally. A sign there is an end in sight. I tell myself to push this last bit and not look down at my watch while I conquer the finish line.

You did it, Alice.

Robert was right; the top of the mountain is beautiful. I'm above the clouds. Looking out at the ocean, I see the pier where I started this morning.

Look how far I've come.

For the first time in a while, I feel strong. Not just the first time from this past week, but I mean truly in a while. I make my way out to a rock that overlooks the city and go to pull out my phone for a quick photo.

"Alice!" my dad interrupts my selfie with his cheering. "Wow, you beat everyone up here? There isn't a person in sight. How do you feel?"

I retrieve the water in his hand. "Honestly, Dad, I feel good. My body refused to stop. It's almost as if I went numb and let the adrenaline carry me up."

We both stand there for a moment, looking out and appreciating the view in front of us.

My dad breaks the silence, "Remember this moment, Alice. You're strong. You're going through hell right now, and look what you did. I wish David understood what he was giving up."

"Yeah, me too."

"I'm proud of you. And you should be proud of yourself."

"Thank you, Dad, and thank you for being here today. I couldn't have done it without your help along the way."

Our conversation stops as Robert, and a few others make their way up the finish line, cheering for the end of the dreadful run. Every person coming up is elated to see the end. It's neat to watch how each person lights up as they near the top and realize what they just accomplished. The energy and camaraderie are contagious.

"Alice, you're already here? You don't even look tired," Rob says, giving me a fist bump.

"Oh, I will be paying for it in the next couple of days, I'm sure. For now, my body is pretty numb."

"Hey, numb or not, that is incredible. Absolutely crushed it like I knew you would," Rob finishes and goes to high five everyone else reaching the top of the mountain.

Something happened today, something I can't quite explain or put my finger on, but it felt like the new start to the rest of my life. One that is created and owned by me. Now I just need to decide what I am going to make of it.

Chapter Seven

"Wait, that did *not* happen. Start from the beginning."

Dev and I are laughing on the back porch of my parent's house, enjoying our second round of margaritas. We are finally getting some alone best friend time, and having her here with me makes me feel whole again. After all, she is my person.

"Alice, I'm serious. I ripped my Lulus. They got caught on a fence and straight ripped. Bare leg and all for the world to see."

Not sure if it's the tequila or the story itself, but we can't stop cackling.

"Okay, but how? Why?"

"Alice, I was *so* stunned when I read your text. First of all, you can't just drop news like that over a text."

"Well, I was in an emotional state, Dev," I say, laughing. "What else do you expect from me?"

"Fair point, but I had to call right away. I mean, when your best friend sends a random text days before her wedding that says '*David ended it, I'm coming home*,' I'm obviously calling you immediately. Gosh, I swear I went into fight or flight mode like a mama bear."

"Yeah, I get that, but why did you run outside?"

"Well, you know I was still visiting with my family, and we were all together in the house. I needed to get out and call you. They were all so worried, too, because my reaction was insane. You should have seen how fast I stormed out, yelling out curse words as I darted for the door."

"You're insane, but I love you for it. Gosh, I barely even remember our conversation that day. It was all such a blur."

"Same here. I ran outside, an absolute hot mess, and then my leggings got caught on this little fence and ripped. There goes $100. So, tell David he also owes me a new pair of leggings. Or, if you want, I can text him and let him know. Along with a few other words I have for that idiot," she exclaims, raising her glass up in the air.

"No, no, not necessary. You, out of everyone, know that it wouldn't serve any purpose. He really is done with me. I haven't even heard more from him."

"Ugh, I wish that wasn't true. Well, I mean, at this point, I am happy you're not with him after seeing his behavior now, but I wish he would reach out and show more remorse."

"I know, me too."

We let the silence of my parent's spacious backyard sit with us for a minute. I could sit out on this back porch swing for hours and get lost in the comfort of this home. Grass runs out about an acre, and the neighbors are far enough to maintain privacy but not feel alone. Childhood memories run through my mind of the chaotic fun we had as kids.

"Have you heard from anyone else?" Dev pulls me out of my gaze. "What about Adam? I feel like he would reach out."

Ever since David and I had started dating, Dev also grew close to his friend, Adam. It was fun having the four of us grow closer. This has been a difficult part of the breakup. I not only lost David but all the people I met through him.

"Nope, nothing from him or anyone on David's side. Well, except for his mom."

"Gosh. Total BS and you know it. I also have a few words for Adam. Can you believe he talked to me on the phone for a whole *two* hours the day before?" Dev discloses. "Do you think Adam knew for a fact he was going to end it?"

"Oh, I'm sure he did," I say, taking another drink of my margarita. "You would know if *I* was about to do something that drastic."

"Girl, I better know, but I wouldn't let you do this to anyone. I would call you out if your character was in question."

"I know. That's why I keep you around. Honesty and endless girl chats over margaritas!"

Clink! Our glasses hit for what is probably our fifth cheers of the evening. This girl's time is so needed. No one knows the depths of your love life like your best friend. Dev has been with me from the start of mine and David's relationship. She also came out to visit us many times and was probably the closest to David out of anyone in my life.

"But honestly, Alice, I can't believe no one has reached out. That is horrible. It was your freaking wedding! Why are they acting so chill about it? I feel like I'm mourning this loss with you. What the heck, people, c'mon." Dev raises her voice.

"Right? I can't help but wonder what he told people. It's weird. Scary almost how fast he has closed this chapter. How quickly he took care of everything. I don't know what to make of it. I just hope people don't think—"

"Alice, you can't care what people think. Focus on you and only you."

"Yes, but I poured my heart into getting to know his people. Learning about their lives, building relationships, and accepting them into my future. I loved him, and I cared for every person that came with him."

There is a moment of stillness after I say this, and I take a few more sips of my margarita. I'm getting ready for another round. I look over at Dev, who is twirling around the ice in her drink. I can tell she is getting ready to say something.

"Do you think he told them they weren't allowed to reach out?" Dev asks.

Oh, wow. This question makes me stop and wonder. I could give everyone the benefit of the doubt and say yes, but then that makes me angrier at David. As if he has the power to control others. But if I say no, then I'm also deeply hurt by the people with who I thought I had developed relationships over the past few years.

What did David say to everyone anyways? Did he tell them he ended it? Did he reveal how out of the blue it was or how he went about it? What about when people ask him how I'm doing? I wonder if he says I'm fine or if he says he doesn't know. I would do anything to know what goes on in his mind.

"At this point, Dev, I have no idea. If I say yes, then it makes me realize how little I knew David and his character, but if I say no, then..."

"I know," she interrupts. "I get it. Let's drop it. How do you feel about the trip to Colorado?"

"Hmm, I don't know. Doesn't feel real. I feel numb," I admit, biting my cheek as I gather my feelings. "It doesn't feel like I'm going back for the reason I am..."

"What do you mean?"

"A part of me, and I know this sounds wild, but a part of me thinks I'll return and go back to my old life. Like David will pick me up from the airport, and I'll recap my trip on our drive home, admire the scenery, and fall back into our usual routine. Do I sound insane for still feeling this way? Or even still longing for that?"

"Absolutely *not*. Alice, this is going to take time. Give yourself credit for how you're handling it so far. I would be in bed, eating ice cream, and sobbing. It's amazing you're even dressed and laughing on this swing with me."

"Ha, hardly."

"And one day, you're going to end up with a guy who sweeps you off your feet and makes you forget all about David."

"Gosh, I can't even think about dating again." I laugh, but really the thought of dating again makes me nervous. When will I be ready? Do I even know how to flirt anymore? All those dates, texting and talking stages, and trying to impress someone. Ugh. Sounds horrible.

"I know, I know. Take your time to get back out there, but you're a hit. So if something happens, I'm just saying, let it happen. Go off and kiss all the boys."

"Dev! You're crazy. I can't even think about kissing someone else."

"You're right. I'm sorry. But I do look forward to our next girl's trip where we bring back *Wild Alice*." She gives a little shoulder shimmy. "I know that side of Alice still lives in there."

"Ha! Again, hardly."

Thinking back to our past girl's trips and times from college, I barely even remember that girl. To be honest, I haven't even had drinks like this in a long time. There was so much I erased and hid from David about my past. He was never too fond of my past, which was nothing to scoff about, but man did he make me feel guilty.

"Fine. I will just say this, and then we can move on," she says, raising her glass for another cheers. "Good riddance because you dodged a massive bullet."

"Dev!"

"What? It's true," she says, taking the final sip of her drink. "Oh wow, I need a refill. Let's go make more."

Chapter Eight

———

The parking garage is dark and quiet. After roaming the crowded airport, it's weird to only hear our suitcases roll on the pavement as we make our way to my car. Being back in Colorado is strange. I thought my feelings would heighten on the flight or even landing in Denver, but it's not until I return to my car that the reality of this trip sinks in.

After playing Tetris to fit all the luggage into my little Hyundai, I'm flushed and ready to get going. We've been up since the crack of dawn, and packing my stuff into suitcases won't be a light task.

As I turn on my car, I see my dashboard is flashing a light. *Frick.* My tire pressure light is on. Stressed, I jump out of the driver's seat and frantically run around the car, surveying all the tires.

"Alice, what are you doing?" my dad asks as he gets out of the car to see what is happening.

"My tire pressure light is on, but nothing looks flat, I just—"

"Alice, it's okay," my dad's voice was fairly calm. "We will stop at the nearest gas station and add some air. This happens from time to time. Come on, let's go get them fixed."

"Okay." I take a deep breath and head back to the driver's seat.

Were already off to an overwhelming start. This week has me so on edge that even the smallest inconveniences will set me off. My goal is to be in and out of this state without any trouble. I'm anxious to get to the storage unit, get my stuff, and leave.

*

After airing up the tires, battling through traffic, and only having consumed coffee in the past twenty-four hours, we arrive at the storage unit. When he sent the location in the email, I knew exactly which one it was. We—well, especially me—drove by this storage place many times. It was on the way to church, Target, and my old apartment. We even had to pass it to get to the Lowe's, where he surprised me with our first *real* Christmas tree.

I am still shocked to this day how much he got into the Christmas spirit that year. Oh man, I will never forget how we squeezed that tree into the back of his little Kia Soul. We were still finding and vacuuming up pine needles months and months later, which is why he made it clear he refused to get a real tree ever again. Another moment where he was a thief of my joy and I allowed it. Maybe it's a silly thing, but he knew the joy Christmas brought me. Denying our apartment the smell of a real tree and the nostalgia of my childhood was cruel. However, this was nonnegotiable for him.

I can't believe I'm here. The memories are fresher than I anticipated.

Everything about this moment makes me want to cry, shut down, and not deal with what is ahead. But having my parents here puts me in work mode. I can't let my guard down.

The whole drive here was uncomfortable. For starters, we are drained and hungry. But as we made our way down the interstate, conversations switched from admiring the beautiful state of Colorado to my parents being absolutely disturbed by the fact David let me drive this freeway alone that day. Lanes are narrow as construction takes place for at least twenty miles. It is riddled with sharp turns, bumpy patches, massive trucks merging in and out, and cars that still drive recklessly.

"I can't get over how beautiful this state is," my mom says as we walk up to the lobby. The storage unit has an obnoxiously gorgeous view of the mountains. "Oh Alice, aren't you the *slightest* bit sad to leave Colorado?"

Can we not?

"Yes, I know it's a beautiful state."

"Sorry, I didn't mean for that to be insensitive. I just wish the circumstances were different. All of this, it's just not fair. This isn't right—" Her words start to break up as I can hear the emotion coming into her words.

This moment is hitting both of us so hard right now. Maybe I should have come alone or just brought Devon. Maybe I should have sucked it up and paid for movers to come to do this. But it's too late for that, so I focus my eyes forward and lead us into the lobby.

"Welcome in. How can I help you?" the employee at the front desk asks.

"Hi, yes, where do I head to access the units?"

Just like that, we are back to getting shit done.

*

"Alice!" my wedding coordinator warmly greets me. She graciously offered her time and car to help me move out.

"Natalie," I say, embracing her. "Thank you for coming. It means so much." I pull back and look at my parents. "Mom and Dad, this is our wedding coordinator, Natalie."

"We have heard such great things about you," my mom says. "Thank you for being here today."

"Absolutely. My heart just broke when Alice told me what happened, I've been in this position before, and I understand the weight of it. A lot of people supported me through my broken engagement, and now it's my turn to help our Alice. This is the least I can do for her."

"Well, thank you again, Natalie." Ushering us back toward the side entrance that leads to our reserved spot, I say, "Shall we?"

I pull out the key and the paper with the code to enter the building that David sent me. He was always good with giving instructions. I have to hand him that. As I finish typing in the code, the screen flashes, *"Welcome, David."*

"Really? He couldn't have changed the name?" mom blurts out, and she's right. I hate that it says his name. Now I have to read that every time we come in and out.

"All right, well, let's just grab some carts and get started," I say, directing everyone.

This place is a creepy maze. My stomach is in knots as I find the unit and get reunited with all my belongings.

When we open the storage unit, everything is placed and organized nicely. Admittedly, he was thoughtful and careful placing my stuff. My wedding dress hangs along the wall so it wouldn't be folded and ruined, hanging at a height only he could reach. Storing my stuff nicely was the least he could do after ignoring my request not to touch my personal belongings.

"Where do you want to start?" my mom asks.

"Yes, just put us to work," my dad continues. "Oh, but first, is the ring in here? He left that for you, right?"

"I don't know. I'm not expecting him to."

"Well, he should. It belongs to you—"

"I don't see it, but I wouldn't know where to even start looking for it. But I also wouldn't expect him to return it at this point."

"What about a note? Do you think he left her anything?" my mom whispers to Amy behind me.

"All right, team, let's get started," I cry, preventing any more side chatter. "Mom and Natalie, can you please fold clothes into my suitcases? And Dad, let's get these larger furniture items down to Natalie's car."

In the next hour, we crank out more work than I anticipated. We load up Natalie's car with everything I need to sell or donate and place wedding gifts in my car to return. Everyone has hustled and kept busy, so we can get out of here as soon as possible. This place gives me the chills. Why are storage units so creepy? The pale walls, quiet halls, and the sound of the garage doors sliding up and down. I'm sure I'm the only one retrieving their belongings from an ex.

At this point, our energy and my patience are running low. I decided to call it a day and advised we go return the wedding gifts.

"All right, is there anything else I can take with me? Or do you need me to come back for more?" Natalie asks as we walk out.

"No, you have done a lot already. Thank you for helping me get items sold and donated. This helps so much. Obviously, I can't bring things like a TV stand back on a flight. Massive weight off our shoulders," I say to her.

"Of course, Alice. Anything. If you ever, and I mean *ever*, need anything, don't hesitate to call me. You're going to be just fine."

Crazy to think how she went from helping me plan my wedding to helping me un-plan the event and pack up my entire life.

*

It has now been a full fourteen hours of travel filled with heavy emotions and lots of moving, and I have yet to feed my parents. Energy is low, and I sense we're all anxious to get food and rest. But since Pottery Barn and Williams Sonoma are on the way to the hotel, I want to knock this task out of the way. As we carry the boxes inside, I can't help but feel an extreme sense of anxiety.

This is what is debilitating about anxiety. Anxiety is a rabbit hole of "what ifs." The situation erodes away my confidence. Fear and uncertainty have found a permanent home in my mind, and I wish I could evict the two emotions.

When we walk in, the employees are clearly overwhelmed by the number of boxes we're carrying to the counter.

"Okay, so I see we have a lot of returns," a young female employee greets me when I reach the counter. "I just want to be clear before we start that we have a strict thirty-day return window. Are these items purchased within that time frame?"

"Hi," I start with, trying to point out that a simple "hello" would have been a better greeting than the one she gave me. "Most of these are not. They're actually gifts from a registry, so I am not looking to get money back. Just store credit is fine. And I have already called your customer service. They said since they are registry items, the returns qualified for store credit."

Yes, ma'am, I did my research before coming here.

"Hmm, you may have been given the wrong information, but let me see what I can do. Can you please unbox every item? Once you are finished, I will start the return. We will also need the name and number of each person who purchased the gift."

I begin unboxing everything and pulling up information about people who purchased the items. It's almost as if every box I open triggers another customer to head to check out. The line behind me continues to grow as I keep ushering people to go ahead of me. I'm in disbelief this woman is making me do this right now.

"I'm having trouble finding this purchase in our system," she says to me on the first item I hand her. "Can you try finding the email that was used to purchase the item?"

Frustration builds. This is why I organized the receipts beforehand, so this wouldn't be a whole big deal. Just take my items back. They no longer hold any meaning.

"Okay, I finally found it," she says the same moment I find the email address she needed. "Just so you know, this will take a while."

"That's okay, I understand." Lie. I'm trying to maintain whatever patience I have left in me.

"Thank you for waiting," she says to the line of customers still waiting behind me.

Could this get any worse?

While I watch her search her system, I eavesdrop on a couple standing at the register next to me. Clearly, newlyweds, they discuss the perfect dinner collection for the upcoming holiday season. Even the store associate checking them out can't help but give me a pity glance. I feel it. Everyone in here is looking at me, listening in on this conversation.

"We usually wouldn't allow returns like this for this reason, just so you know." She looks up and says to me, "*So*, what is even the reason for the return? Did you not like the items?"

"No, it's not that."

"Okay, well, I need to type in a reason for the system to approve the return," she interrupts and darts her eyes back at me.

"Well, they were wedding gifts—"

"And you and your spouse don't want them anymore?" she asks while continuing to type away.

"No, it's not that."

She looks back up at me, waiting for my answer. Why does this even matter?

"There isn't a wedding anymore. It's not happening. That's why," I say, snapping back.

Her jaw drops. "Oh, I'm so—I'm sorry, I didn't know—" Finally, some compassion and kindness.

"It's fine. I just need to return these gifts." This is exactly what I don't want. The sorrow and apologies don't mean much if I can't even get it from my own ex-fiancé.

She is now moving faster to get the returns processed and smiles each time she hands back a receipt. I wish my parents would've stayed in the car instead of coming in to witness this public humiliation.

All the items thoughtfully selected for our kitchen, bathroom, and every room in our future home lie before me. I watch them slowly get stacked and thrown into a pile. I've envisioned holidays and dinner parties that would be hosted with these glasses and dinnerware but never did I once imagine being in this spot. After the last return, my parents and I finally head out.

"Alice, your dad and I are in awe of how well you carry yourself. Your strength today and in that store," she pauses for a moment, still wrapping her head around everything we are dealing with, "I can't imagine how difficult that was, but you wouldn't know it with how tall and strong you stood."

This time I don't say anything back, but I give a smile. The affirmations from everyone are sweet, but at this point, I'm getting tired of them; I want this all behind me.

I put the car in reverse and headed for the hotel. One day down.

Chapter Nine

It's amazing how much you can achieve when you are under the pressure of time. My parents left earlier this week, and I dropped them off with seven suitcases filled to the brim with my belongings. Then I picked up Dev, who flew in to help me with the rest of the to-do list for my time in Colorado, along with a few nights out to mask the other memories this place holds for me. I can't believe we emptied that storage unit and fit everything into suitcases.

This was just one aspect of the week. I also sold my car and cleared out my desk at work. My manager was kind enough to give me another month to work remotely, but after that, I will have to decide if I plan to return back to Colorado or leave the company. As for my car, it was time I parted ways and started fresh.

"How are you feeling?" Dev asks as we buckle our seats on the plane. "You seem quiet this morning."

This is the question I get asked about five times a day from Dev, my mom, my sister, and anyone else who knows my situation. I'm tired. That's how I'm feeling. Also, I can't believe that I just once *again* packed up my whole life and moved out of another state. It was only fourteen months ago that I had a huge sendoff when I left California to move to Colorado for David and our relationship. Now I'm back to square one.

"I'm good, just tired," I say, hoping it's enough to hold her over for a while.

The plane feels exceptionally warm today, and everyone is taking forever getting settled in their seats. Anxious to get home, my patience with travel is running thin. After twenty minutes of passengers boarding and situating their luggage, we are finally headed for the runway. My body feels uncomfortable. I can't seem to find a spot to help me relax. Suddenly it feels nearly impossible to breathe. My armpits are sweating. My legs are shaking. I'm desperate for water, anything to help my dry throat.

As the plane starts angling upward, it hits me. This is the end. Colorado, this chapter of my life, is done.

Earlier this week, I calculated how many times I have traveled back and forth for David. Twenty-four. Twenty freaking four trips in and out of this airport for our relationship and life here. This was my new home, my new beginning, the future David and I dreamed up together. And now, in a total of six hundred pounds worth of luggage, that future is packed up and going home to live with my parents.

Squeezing my eyes tight, I try my best to hold it all in.

Here we go.

Dev takes notice and pulls out a tissue. She pulls me closer and lets me release the feelings I have held in all week long. Crying on a plane out of Colorado is all too familiar. Passengers do their best not to stare, as I give a sad attempt to stay composed. The more I try to conceal it, the worse it gets. Thankfully I have a friend with me once again.

It takes some time for me to pull it together. Each time I thought I was okay, my body would let go again.

"Alice, what happened?" Dev finally asks when I've caught my breath. "Are you okay?"

"Sorry. The weight of this hit me. It's really over."

"Yes, it is." She pauses as I blow my nose, using my sweatshirt sleeve to wipe my eyes.

"And now what? I leave. He stays here. We never speak again?"

"I'm so sorry, Alice. I wish I knew what to say. I wish I could give you the clarity he failed to give you."

"No, no, it's okay. This is on him, not you. It's fine."

"I know, but this is also a new beginning. Something better is out there for you. I feel it."

"Thank you. Gosh, I'm so sorry to do this in public. So embarrassing for you to deal with this."

"First of all, who gives a shit what other people think? Second of all, no one gives a shit. And third of all, a part of me is relieved to see you cry. It's been a while since I've seen you cry; I never could really tell what was going on in your head. So this is good. This is healthy. This is normal. It is okay to cry. Alice, you have got to remember to express those feelings."

"I know. But it's hard for me. David didn't cry. Every time I do, I feel like an idiot crying over a man who didn't cry when he left me."

"Okay, do you want me to share my thoughts on that whole situation again or—"

"No," I laugh, remembering our conversation when I replayed how David acted the day of our breakup. "One time was enough."

"Alice, people admire you, and you have inspired us all with your strength. Watching you this week was unreal. From the storage unit to selling your car and braving your coworkers as you shared the news. It was unbelievable. I know you.

You'll find a way to turn this into something better: a future you actually want and deserve."

Dev is ready to go down a spiral of inspirational talk that I quite frankly am not in the mood for, but we are interrupted by a man sitting next to us.

"I'm so sorry to interrupt," he says, his southern accent thick. "But I overheard you, and I wanted to say I'm so sorry. Here are some more tissues and water if you need them. I know it may be a while before the attendants make it over to us."

"Oh my gosh, thank you. *I'm* sorry I disrupted your flight. I promise it won't happen again," trying to make light of this chat.

"Never be sorry for this. So where are y'all from?"

"California," Dev and I say.

"Ah, good ole California girls. I had a feeling."

"What about you?" I ask.

"Nashville. Nashville, Tennessee. Greatest city ever. You ever been?"

"No, never been, but I've always wanted to visit. Seems like the perfect place for a slower pace of life while still having access into the city." I really could envision myself being in Nashville.

"Oh yeah," he affirms. "It's perfect. Best of both worlds."

"So, what brought you to Colorado?"

"Ah, my nephew. He's on this flight, actually but got seated back by the bathrooms. And I love the son of a gun, but not enough to sit near a bathroom for a flight. Y'all hear me? Well, anyways, we had a layover in Denver but are headed to California for some business work and to meet with a few vendors. He just opened a coffee shop in Nashville. He's a good fella. Invited me to join because I had never been. So I told the wife to watch the over the chickens and goats while I explored them California beaches."

His accent! I can't get over it. It's so sweet. My heart melts.

"Aww, well, how nice of him to include you. I'm certain you'll love it."

"Thank you, ma'am," he tips his hat and continues. "Well, I won't bother you, ladies, too much, but if you need more tissues, just holler at me. I need to rest before the California party begins."

Turning to Dev, I say, "I think I have some research to do when I get home."

Chapter Ten

NINE MONTHS LATER

Screeeech.

Ugh, this darn door. It must have some sort of sick radar on it. Anytime I try to sneak back into the apartment late at night, it makes the loudest noises possible. It brings me back to high school when I would sneak back into the house. On very few occasions, of course. I was well-behaved 90 percent of the time. Shutting the door slowly seems to only make it worse.

"I hear you... Just shut the door already," Chelsea yells while making her way into our living room. "So another late date, huh? Was this with Kyle again?"

My roommate Chelsea is great, but this girl is nosey and keeps tabs like no other. I thought living with a random person meant we would keep our lives separate, but *separate* isn't really a concept Chelsea lives by.

"No, not Kyle, he was last night. Tonight was Josh," I shamelessly admit thanks to the margaritas from tonight.

"Geez, Alice, I can't keep track of your packages or your men at this rate. Speaking of which, you got another package. What did you order from Revolve?" Chelsea walks out wearing a cat pajama onesie that inch well up above her ankles. She is six feet tall and as slender as they come. Gah, I would kill for her long, lean legs. But on the plus side, I've never had to worry about her stealing my clothes.

"Well, for starters, you don't need to keep track of either, thank you very much." Snatching the package from her hand, "And second, yay, you know I love getting my packages! Gimme gimme!"

Online shopping is frequent nowadays. After the breakup, I did a massive clean out of my closet and belongings. Anything that reminded me of David was thrown out. And I mean anything. From outfits on special occasions to any article of clothing I remember wearing in front of him. If he saw it, it was trash to me.

"So, tell me, how was the date? Is he a keeper? What did you guys do?" Chelsea follows me back to my room as she makes herself comfortable on my desk chair.

"First of all, Josh is hot." Slipping on my new jacket from Revolve. "And we went to Top Golf which, by the way, what is the obsession with Top Golf here in Nashville? This is the second date I've been on with a guy who took me there, and I know the staff is going to start judging me if I go back a third time with a different guy."

"I don't know. The men I date don't take me golfing. Do you know where you should go for a date? Slam Poetry. It's so passionate and exhilarating."

"Yeah, maybe."

When I started my plan to move to Nashville, I thought about living alone. But for starters, it was expensive, and also, I wanted to make friends. So I found a website that pairs compatible people. Chelsea is great, and we match well on a roommate basis, but she is an odd cookie in the best way possible.

Spinning around in my jacket, I ask, "How does this look?"

"Hmm." She looks me up and down. "I would say it's definitely more Alice than Chelsea, so it's perfect for you," she shares, which I know is her way of saying she would never wear it. This tells me I should keep it.

"Well, you know I am trying to rebuild my closet, and I think this jacket will be a staple. Plus, it screams Nashville," I say, rubbing my hand on the soft blue leather jacket. It's chic with a modern, Western look that would get compliments in any bar.

"I know. I still can't believe how little clothing and items you had when you moved in. Why was that?"

"Just didn't have much."

"Mm, no. You *obviously* love clothes. For someone who is clearly a shopaholic, there has to be a reason you left so much behind." Chelsea points out.

"Chels, it's a long story, and it's late."

"Ah, does this revolve around the mysterious breakup? When are you ever going to tell me about that?" Chelsea crosses her arms. "I'll be honest, I've tried to dig through your social media for answers but—nothing. I have nothing."

Her frustration makes me laugh. This gives me a sense of accomplishment because that means I did a good job erasing everything of David and our relationship from my profiles. It also helped that he doesn't have social media. Keeps everything on the down low. When I said Nashville would be a fresh start, I meant it.

"You'll hear about it one day. You just have to wait." I make my way out to the bathroom to brush my teeth and get ready for bed.

"What does that mean? You know roommates usually tell each other things." Chelsea trails closely behind me.

"Chels, relax. You'll see."

"Okay, but what does that mean? *'I'll hear about it one day,'*" she mocks with air quotes. "Can't I get a hint?"

"No. Now I have to go to bed. Early wake-up call for a training run. Good night. Oh! And stop going through my mail," I say lightheartedly as I close the bathroom door.

"Ha ha. And you stop dating every guy you meet. Then maybe you'll be home to get the mail on your own," Chelsea jokes back through the door.

We may be a little different, but at least she knows how to mess around. I lucked out with this roommate.

*

Last night's margaritas and endless chips and guac are the epitome of my discomfort right now. At five miles into my run, I'm almost to my halfway point. I'm dreading saying yes to a third round of drinks with Josh. Although the date was fun. No regrets on getting out. I just wish I hadn't the night before a training run. I should know better.

Stopping to catch my breath and grab some water, I see a text from Josh. It's the classic "had a great time, when can I see you again?" kind of text.

Josh was fun, but he was too flirty in a cliché way that made him feel like just another guy. Like the time he stepped up to "help" my golf swing just so he had an excuse to get close and hug me from behind. Guys like him are fun for a few dates, but they're hoping to score by date three at least. Especially when he let me drink that much on our first date. He isn't looking to get to know me. The guy even tried to share an Uber back to my place. He clearly isn't looking to settle down, and I'm not looking to hook up with someone I know won't lead to anything.

I put my phone back in my waistband pack and keep trekking forward. The quick break was much needed, and I'll admit seeing Josh's text gave me a little bit of an ego boost. Feels good to be pursued.

"Coming up on your left," a man behind me shouts as he passes me with his adorable Australian Shepherd. People here have the best manners. Back in California, you were expected to know when to move out of someone's way or else risk being plowed over. Unlike here in the South, where strangers smile as they pass you, they call you ma'am, and the men almost always rush up to open doors for you. I love it.

"Oof," I say, startled at first. "Thanks, good morning!" I respond with a smile and a quick wave.

"Good morning to you too," he turns to run backward for a split second, getting another look at me.

Wow, that was smooth. My goodness, that man is fit and *hot*. Sheesh. But before I can say anything else, he continues forward. This is my cue to focus and turn up the dial. The options of men here in Nashville are endless. It's a sea of handsome guys everywhere I go, and their Southern hospitality is such a contrast from the men in California. Moving away from everything back home was the right decision.

*

As I get to my car, I rest my arms on top of my head. I am longing, no, desperate for more water. Alcohol dried my body up, and I ran out of water about two miles back. Hopefully, I still have extra bottles in the back of my car.

When I turn to open my door, I see the sweet Australian Shepherd and its owner standing next to my door. This guy is even cuter the second time around.

"Hi, sorry," I point at my car. "Can I squeeze by?"

He looks up from his phone, and I get a better look at him. Tall. I would say at least six foot three. Dark features and a chiseled jawline. Sweat around the neck of his shirt to show he worked out but was clearly in good shape, so it must have been easy for him. His clothes fit him nicely, and his style is impeccable. Lululemon head to toe with matching running shoes. Have mercy! My kind of guy.

"Oh yes, excuse me, sorry. I can get so distracted by this device," he says, lifting up his phone and then ushering his arm forward as if he's giving me permission to my car. Makes me chuckle a little.

"How was your run?" the man continues as I reach into my center console, putting my earbuds away.

"It was, um—" I'm scouring my car for an extra bottle of water, and I interrupt my own response back to him. "Ugh, are you kidding me?"

"Who, me?" he asks, "You good over there?"

"Sorry, yes, I thought I had another water waiting for me, and I don't. But um… My run, it was um, good. Well, rough. A good rough. Sorry, I'm very dehydrated, so—" I'm wiping my face with my shirt, completely drenched in sweat. Why do I have to meet this man now?

"Here, I have an extra," he says, handing me a bottle.

"Oh wow, thank you, are you sure?"

"You need it more than me." He's laughing as he lets his dog back in his car. "Have a good one. See you around!"

What? That's it? I didn't even get to pet the dog.

As I watch him drive off through my rearview mirror, I take note he drives an Audi. *Sheesh.* Cute guy, adorable dog, nice manners, *and* a fancy car? A man who clearly has it all.

My drive home is quieter than usual. I don't belt out music as I'm lost in my thoughts about this man. Did he have a ring? I should have looked more closely. Honestly, with him being *that* good-looking, he is probably married or dating someone. That level of attractiveness likely steals the attention of any room he walks in. Almost too good to be true. I wonder how often he comes to this spot. Next time I "see him around," I'll be better prepared.

*

My bed is soaking wet as I throw the covers off. My alarm hasn't even sounded off yet. Not only is the humidity here in the South intense for a California girl, but ever since the breakup, night sweats have become an unfortunate pattern as dreams of David linger. These dreams aren't as frequent as the first three months after the breakup. Back then, it was almost every night.

At night I would be so exhausted from working to keep a smile on my face all day. As soon as I would lie in bed, tears would fall. These pent-up emotions would then bleed into my dreams, and I could never fully escape. But the dreams weren't always sad. Every now and then, I dreamed about him coming back for me. Even apologizing. Other times it would be us having a good time with no mention of a breakup. Those were the ones I would force myself back asleep, never wanting them to end. But last night wasn't fun, hence the sweaty bed.

The setting was not anywhere familiar. An older church held all my belongings. David ended things not only with me but with his family. He was ready to ship me, my things, and his family out. He even began to pack up my stuff for me while I begged him not to leave.

Lying in bed, I opened my phone notes app and typed out the dream, an exercise my new therapist I started seeing encouraged me to do to help process this time of grief. Plus, the notes are not only beneficial for my therapist to understand what I experienced, but they're also great anecdotes for the book I'm writing.

With all the downtime I had living back at home, I started to write. At first, it was therapeutic to just journal, but since then, it's turned into more of a serious project. Writing a book has always been a dream of mine. So why not turn this experience into something entertaining?

I should have known better than to start writing in my notes section before work because I'm late and running fifteen minutes behind schedule. Once I start writing out my thoughts, it's hard to stop. Now I'm racing to pull myself together to get to work on time, so I throw my hair back in a bun and get moving.

After leaving Colorado, I fought hard to keep my job, but they needed my position to be in the office. As much as I tried to picture myself moving back to Colorado, it was too hard to bear. Everything about that state reminds me of him, of us. So I decided to quit and find a new job in Nashville. This new job isn't like the leadership role I had at my old company, but it's with one of the top global marketing companies I've always dreamed of working at.

It may not be the same pay or position, but the perks are great. They allow for flexible remote working hours, which helps when I have therapy or want to take a break and work from a coffee shop.

Ping ping.

Dev: *Hi! Since you said you didn't have a preference on what date I flew into Nashville, I went ahead and booked a trip. Forwarded the booking confirmation to your email. Thinking of you and can't wait to hug you!*

Ping ping, another text from Dev.

Dev: *Also, don't think I can't see you starting to type and then stop. It's been a few days since I have heard from you. Can we set up a phone date? I feel like I know* nothing *about your life in Nash. I'm becoming a jealous bff.*

Laugh at her subtle dig. Between dating, writing a book, training for a race, working, and finding my way around Nashville, I have been a little MIA. Plus, every time we talk, she always wants to talk about how I'm feeling. No, thank you.

Me: *You are such a drama queen in the mornings. Also, I can't believe you are up so early! What is it, 5 a.m. over there? Saw the confirmation email. I can't wait! Let's chat this weekend.*

I throw my phone in my bag and spritz on some perfume. I go from being fifteen minutes behind to two minutes ahead of schedule. I give myself one last look in the mirror.

If there is anything I learned from my run the other day, it's that you never know who you might meet or run into.

Chapter Eleven

Riding the wave of my runner's high from this morning, I'm reminded that my body is getting stronger, and my pace is faster. There was a spark that set off inside me from the race in Santa Barbara I ran with Robert. It kickstarted this desire to run more than I had been. Since then, I signed up for my first marathon and haven't stopped.

Running is a way for me to get out and be alone. Here in Nashville, I can enjoy the fresh air and green trails that carry me for miles. Depending on the day, my playlist might match what I'm feeling. Some days it's old-school hip hop. Other days it's worship music. Whatever it takes to push through the hurt and go the distance. Propelling through the runs reminds me I can fight through hard emotions.

Not that David can see me or that he cares, but there is still this feeling inside me that I need to prove to him, and anyone else in my life for that matter, that I am doing *okay*. No one needs to worry. I have control over my life. There is nothing he or anyone else can take away from me anymore. But what if one day mine and David's paths cross? I want to look good. No, look better. Make him regret his decision.

Living in Nashville has given me the freedom to start fresh. I can avoid the day-to-day questions about how I am feeling and people who watch my every move. It's interesting how many people will tell you to *"take your time with healing"* or "*do what is best for you.*" At the same time, other folks ask, "*when do you think you'll move on and date again?*" Or share their opinion that I "*moved to a new city too fast.*"

There is a constant tug of war inside me. I do my best not to let the opinions or questions of others get to me, but there are moments where I wonder if, at some point, all the excitement and big changes in my life will catch up to me. Riding a wave of fun and new opportunities can only last so long, but I refuse to be that girl who wallows in self-pity. Before I head inside my apartment, I open up Instagram and share a selfie to my story. I caption it "Saturday Morning Grind" with a muscle emoji, and I swipe until I find the right filter—*perfect!*

Making my way to the shower, I turn on my "Feel Good" playlist as I start stripping off the sweaty gear. I start dancing and admire the progress my body has made. My hairbrush becomes my mic, and I whip my shirt in the air as the steam from the shower starts to cloud over the curtain. This is my cue to get in and get on with the day.

As I let the water roll down my skin, feeling the sweat drip away, I continue moving to the music. I can't help but think back to David and how embarrassed he was when I would dance. He would scoff and say things like, "please don't do that ever again," and I would roll my eyes as if I didn't care but would always stop.

These are the moments where I miss my old self slightly more than I miss him.

As I hop out of the shower, I take my time getting ready and picking out the perfect Saturday casual outfit. Fitted ankle booties, my favorite light-wash straight jeans, a black blouse, and a belt to tie it all together. I tuck in my blouse, an Alice-style standard. I throw my curled hair into a high pony and add thick, gold hoops. I'm feeling powerful.

"Where are you headed? Another date?" Chelsea pops her head into the bathroom.

"No, just channeling my inner boss girl," I say, giving her a quick smirk. "I need to head to a coffee shop to get some work done. Hey, do you have any recommendations? The one I went to last week had *such* watered-down coffee, and the men there weren't even cute."

"Hmm, have you been to Good & Gather yet?"

"No, I haven't."

"What!" she cries, cutting me off. "You have to go. It's the best. And the staff there are *so* great. I wish I could join you, but I am volunteering at the local theater today to help set up for their next performance of Shakespeare's *As You Like It.* You should totally stop by after working."

"Yeah, maybe..." I say noncommittally as I scroll Good & Gather's Instagram to see what the vibe is like. Modern photos, lots of windows for natural lighting, and so many customers with smiley faces.

"Okay, cool, this place looks great. I have to run. Thanks for the rec, Chels. See you later!"

*

"Welcome!" a kind woman shouts behind the espresso machine as I walk in. I'm hooked by the sound of coffee beans grinding and comforted by the addicting aroma of caffeine. I scan the shop for the best place to sit, a coffee shop rule I made for myself. Claim your table before you order. Otherwise, you could end up with a coffee in hand and no place to dine.

Ooh. A corner bar spot with the perfect amount of natural light next to the window is screaming my name. Since it's a bar, I can rotate between sitting and standing. I set down my belongings, place my coat on the chair, and turn for the counter.

"Oh man, good thing you saved your spot," another barista says. His odd, sly smile spreads while he makes someone's latte.

"Well, you just never know," I reply, playing into his teasing. "I mean, I tried to call earlier for reservations, but you guys were booked."

"Yeah, you're lucky you got a spot. This place will be packed in a few minutes. Hottest bar in town."

"Happy I got here in the nick of time." Looking up at the chalk menu board, I say, "It's really just a quirk of mine. I like to make sure I snag a comfy spot to focus before I order."

"Oh, sorry, ma'am, but absolutely not. There will be no focusing and feeling comfortable here."

Oh gosh, wait, he is still joking, right?

"I'm kidding. Just giving you a hard time because it's your first time here."

"Wait, how do you know—"

"I just know," he says, smiling as he cuts me off.

"What gave it away?" I ask, also hoping I haven't accidentally met this guy before.

"Well, for starters, you paused at the door for a solid thirty seconds and debated a table to sit at. Truly just froze there. I've never seen anyone put so much thought into a seating decision. But more importantly, you didn't say 'Hi, Wes' when you walked up to the register. Our customers usually do this because they like me so much. So I'll let it slide this once." He gives me a wink.

Wow, this barista. He seems a little full of himself. I can't decide if he is actually full of himself or just being playful.

"Wes?"

"Or Weston. I go by either."

"I'll stick with Wes."

"Works for me."

"Well, Wes, if the coffee is good enough for me to return one day again, I'll consider greeting you at the door. But no promises."

"Hey, that's all we ask here at Good & Gather—treat the baristas like customers, ya know?" he smiles and continues. "I'm just joking. It's great to have new faces, especially yours. What can I get you started with?"

Oh my. That was smooth.

"Iced vanilla oat milk latte."

"And a name for the drink?" Wes asks.

"Iced vanilla oat milk latte."

Wes lets out a laugh, "Good one, but I was hoping to get your name."

See barista boy, I can make corny jokes too.

Laughing with him, I say, "Right, right, right, my name is—"

"Wait!" he sharply cuts me off. "Let's do this. If you like the drink, you have to come back and share your name before you leave, deal?"

"Wes, I can just tell you my name right now."

"Nope, I kind of want to earn it. Plus, then you have to come back and talk to me." He starts on the espresso machine.

"Deal." I pull out my wallet.

"Nope, don't worry about that either. First-time customer. It's on the house. If you like it, you'll be returning, and that's really all I ask."

Now I understand why Chelsea recommended this shop. The staff is warm and friendly, maybe even a little too friendly.

Do they actually give free drinks to every first-time customer?
Or am I special?

"What? No, that is crazy. Please let me pay." I'm forcing my credit card at him.

"No, I insist. Trust me. Something tells me this won't be your last time here."

When he's not looking, I drop a five in the tip jar and strut back to my chair. *Was he flirting? Okay, maybe I do look really good today. Or does he do that with every girl?*

Alice, stop.

Men can be friendly, and it doesn't have to mean anything. It wouldn't matter anyways. Wes isn't my type. For starters, he's a barista, and that is not a good source of income. I need someone driven and successful. He also isn't six feet tall and has more facial hair than I am used to. Not to mention the very noticeable tattoos on his left arm. Not that I am opposed to tattoos, but I've never really dated a guy with a sleeve of tattoos. I tried to catch a few of them, but the only ones that stuck out were a cross and some forest-looking tree.

Although his smile is adorable, and his style isn't terrible. But he was way too flirty with me as a first-time customer. So I can't help but wonder if he does this with every girl who walks through the door. The last thing I need to entertain is the idea of a guy who I can't trust not to flirt with every girl.

Okay. This needs to stop. Alice, you're thinking about this too much; he's just a barista.

"One iced vanilla oat milk latte." Wes catches me off guard. "So, what are you working on that requires so much focus?" He sits on the chair next to me.

"Nothing!" I slam my laptop fast as I realize I'm on a chapter titled "Sexy Without the Sex."

"Really? It looked like some kind of writing."

"I mean, yes, it's a book... Or it will be a book. I don't know. I'm still working on it."

"Very cool. What's it about?"

"Oh, see, that's a secret. You still have to learn my name. Baby steps, Wes, baby steps."

"All right, mysterious woman, I will leave you to it then. Enjoy the coffee. I look forward to learning your name."

As he gets up, I overhear him greeting a cute, young gal who just walked in. They immediately embrace one another, and as soon as I see her play with her hair, I realize I was right. Wes does flirt with everyone.

I still love the attention, though. It feels nice.

*

Three hours have passed, and my creativity is hitting a wall. I'll admit it did take me about thirty minutes to get settled after my conversation with Wes. Something about him... It was different. Maybe it's because he is so different from the guys I usually flirt with. As I zip up my laptop case, I turn around toward the counter and see Wes standing there drying a glass. We instantly make eye contact.

"Leaving so soon?" he asks, setting the glass down and throwing the dishtowel over his shoulder.

"So soon? Ha! I need to give my eyes a break from the screen," I say, making my way to the counter.

"Fair enough. So let's hear it. What's your name?"

"Confident, are we? How do you know I liked it that much?"

"Trust me. I know the effect my lattes have on people."

"Fine, Wes," rolling my eyes, "I'll hand it to you. The latte was perfect, and that's not just because it was free. Although it helped a little."

"Good, good. And your name?"

"Alice."

"Alice," he says slowly and mouths it a few times to himself as if he is letting it soak in before he speaks. "Alice. It fits you perfectly. I see it."

"Phew! Good to know. I'm sort of stuck with it. In the best way, of course."

"So, Alice, when will I see you again? Assuming you live here, yes?"

"I do live here. I'm somewhat new to Nashville. And yes, this place was great. I can't believe I hadn't heard of it yet."

"Yeah, it's mostly a place only locals know of. We don't have the trendy wall murals that most tourists gravitate toward."

"Those are overrated anyways."

"Well, thank you, that is much appreciated. Have a good day, Alice. See you soon."

"You too!" I say on my way out. I'm dying to turn around and see if he is watching me leave.

Wes gives me these unknown flutters in my body. Is it his mannerisms? His confidence? He does have a charming smile. That alone can win me over. But I remind myself again he is a barista and just doing his job. Countless times I caught him chatting with other female customers.

Hmm. Let me call Dev and get her opinion. We are due for a weekly check-in today anyways. Being long-distance from my best friend is so hard. I love this new city and new beginning, but I can't count the times I have desperately wished Dev was here for every moment. Coming home to fill in Chelsea on my dates isn't quite the same.

Gosh, I hope Wes is not watching me through the window right now. He probably thinks I'm a mess fumbling through my purse, searching for my keys with my phone between my ear and shoulder.

Smash!

My lack of awareness of my surroundings suddenly sends my laptop straight to the ground as I bump into a man who must've also not been paying attention. Shit. The sound of my computer crashing down pierces through my ears.

"Whoa, hey there," the man says as he looks up from his phone. Ha, I was right. He was clearly not paying attention. But when our eyes meet, something in his demeanor changes. It relaxes. "Oh, I'm so sorry. I wasn't paying attention. Are you okay?" He bends down to help grab my laptop.

As he hands me my computer, we both do a double take. Almost as if having this in-sync deja vu moment. At the same time, it clicks for both of us. We know each other.

"Hey, you're dehydration girl, right?" he says with a little finger point.

Ah, the guy who gave me water after my run the other day. Oh my gosh, he already looked so good then, but now he is in business attire, and I'm drooling on the inside. How can someone look *this* hot in dress pants?

"Right. I mean, yes, that's me. I'm not always dehydrated like that, but yes, thank you again. You saved me that day." My words could not sound more choppy.

"Glad to hear that. But how about your stuff? Is your computer okay?" He points to my laptop wrapped tightly in my arms now.

"Oh yeah, I am fine," I say, waving my arm. "I mean, my stuff is fine. My computer, yes, it's okay. It's really no biggie."

Lies. It would be a big deal if this cracked. I cannot afford to buy another computer, having sacrificed only eating beans & rice for a few weeks to help save up for this one.

"Well, here," he ushers to one of the tables outside the shop, "Please check it. I would feel horrible if it broke."

Aw, he cares. First the water, now this? His words feel nonnegotiable. The same way he spoke when giving me water after my run. So I open the laptop and move the mouse around, proving all is well.

"Good as new." Our smiles match when I look back up at him.

"Great. Can't interfere with a hardworking girl like yourself."

"Totally. Well, I'll see you—"

"Look, I know you're heading out, but I would like to make it up to you. Maybe treat you to coffee... Or more water at the very least." His joke makes me laugh. "So, what do you say?"

I'm absolutely thrown off. Just moments ago, I was curious about Wes, but now this guy is back. Whatever is in the air, I'm here for it.

"Oh, yeah, defs!" *Defs? Alice, no. Act smarter, more mature. Look at this man.* "I mean, sure. Not defs."

He laughs and offers his hand out. "My name is Jax, by the way."

"Alice."

"All right, Alice, here is my business card. Give me a text or call, and we will set something up. I look forward to seeing you."

"You too!" I take his card.

Hustling to my car, I hit "Call Dev" on my Bluetooth screen.

"Hey, lady, what's up?" Dev says.

"Dev! Remember the cute man from my run last week?"

"Yes, why? Is he now another man in your life? Geez, what is in the water over there in Nashville? It is truly raining men for you!"

"Yeah, but this one, well, you need to see for yourself. Here, let me send a picture of his business card, and you can work your internet FBI magic. His name appears to be Jaxson, but he goes by Jax."

It takes about thirty seconds for Dev to find him on the internet and uncover all his social media accounts. Apparently, he is a big-time realtor, hence the weekend workwear. It also explains the nice Audi he drives. It turns out he is big in local ministry work through his church, so a strong Christian man as well.

Sounds like a man who is checking every box off my list again. Another too-good-to-be-true kind of man that gives me an all too familiar feeling, but this time it has to be different.

Chapter Twelve

How is Sunday already here? I slept in past my alarm this morning, and I'm racing to shave my legs so I can wear a dress to church with Jax.

This past week was busy. Between working extra hours and my first date with Jax, I'm wiped. Our date was casual, just coffee, but not at Good & Gather. Not that I care what Wes thinks, but I wanted us to have more privacy.

Coffee went well. We talked about our career goals, faith, and what music we liked—covering all the basics of a first date. After our time together, Jax asked if I would join him for church this Sunday. It feels pretty fast to bring a new girl to your church, but I decide to push out the doubt.

In between the chaos of this week, I still made it into Good & Gather twice. First on Tuesday to grab a coffee on the way into work, which Wes was nowhere to be found. Then again, yesterday to spend my afternoon writing. Finally, I saw Wes again. We talked nonsense for about thirty minutes. He is so easy to talk to. I can understand why customers love coming in to visit him.

It's not that a man like Jax doesn't entice me. Rather, the thought of entering another serious relationship terrifies me. The kind of questions he asked, inviting me to church, and talking about what he wants in his future signals he is looking for a serious partner. Jax knows what he wants, and we both sat there at coffee, seeing how well the other person checked off boxes.

I know this because I've been here before. But I can't say no to this man. Guys like Jax don't come around often, and he seems to have it all. I can't give up without giving it a proper shot.

Ouch! Oh crap! Blood runs down the back of my knee from shaving. I'm distracted from my thoughts, and I need to pull it together. I don't want to be late for Jax.

Nothing stands out as I stand in front of my closet. After five different try-ons, my bed is covered in outfits I loved on other days but hate today.

Ping ping. I see Jax's name light up my screen right under the *exact* time he said he would pick me up. Why must he be so on time? Can I ever meet a guy who does not have their shit together and doesn't do what they say they'll do? I mean, truly, what does a girl have to do to find a guy who runs a couple of minutes late?

Jax: *Just pulled in!*

Me: *Hey! Sorry, running a little late this morning. Give me five minutes.*

Jax: *K.*

K? K with a period? Am I crazy, or does that feel cold? Either way, I don't waste any more time curling my hair and instead pull it back into a low bun. I'm rushing to assemble myself as much as I can before heading out the door. I walk to his car promptly five minutes late, and I notice he doesn't get out to open my door like he did after our first hangout.

Deep breath, it's okay. It probably doesn't mean anything.

"Hey, good morning!" I say as I sit in his luxurious car. The leather seats feel amazing, and it still has a new car smell.

"Hey!" His response doesn't offer eye contact as he starts backing out immediately. I look down and notice the two coffee cups in the center console.

"Ooh, one of these for me? Handsome church date and coffee? Thank you, Jesus!" Playfully trying to take his guard down.

"Yeah, I was running early and also made sure I would have enough time to pick one up for you." Again, no eye contact, and I feel terrible. I don't know Jax that well, but anyone in this situation would be able to sense how bothered he is by my lateness.

"Hey, I'm sorry I was running late. Sounds silly, but today is a beautiful day, and I just couldn't decide between a skirt or a dress, and you always look so well put together. I mean, look at you. It's like a walking GQ front cover. I want to impress you and your community at church, so I'm sorry." I'm disappointed in myself for caving so fast when he's being so cold. Church would feel much longer if we don't clear the air now, so it's better if I apologize.

He starts to grin, but it's not for a few seconds until he turns to face me.

Finally.

"Thank you for saying that," he says as he put his hand on my leg. "I don't mean to be cold, but I *do* struggle with people being late, and I don't want to be frustrated with you. So then I was getting frustrated with myself for being frustrated with you," he lets out a deep sigh. "I was trying to calm myself down before you got in the car, and that's why I didn't open your door."

It's an apology, but it still feels a little crazy he is *this* upset about it.

Let it go, Alice. Let it go.

"And you do look nice. Guess the extra minutes were worth it." He looks over at me. "I'm happy you went with the dress. Your legs look amazing. I almost want to send you back home to put on jeans so no one else can enjoy them," Jax says while squeezing my hand a little bit tighter.

Total mood change, but I'll take it. Especially coming from someone as attractive as Jax; my face flushes at this compliment. I reach for my coffee and see the Good & Gather logo.

"Thank you for this, by the way!"

"Of course. I wasn't sure what to get you, so I told the barista to make his favorite drink as long as it included oat milk. You mentioned that our first date, right?"

"Mm, yes!" I'm relishing my first sip. "An oat milk latte with a touch of vanilla, my favorite."

I wonder if Wes made this?

"Do you always get those? You should drink coffee black like me. It's healthier."

"Eh, life is too short. I want to enjoy my coffee."

"Well, I'm just saying, food for thought. We'll get you there one day."

"Jax," I say, looking over at him, "Let's talk about something else. Tell me about your church, tell me about your weekend, tell me more about you."

"All right, I get it. I'll let it go," Jax says. "You're so chill compared to me. It's refreshing and challenging all at once."

*

As the church service wraps up, I'm dying to use the restroom. I ditch Jax as soon as I have the chance, and as I walk away, I see an older couple approaching him. In the bathroom, I take a moment to check myself in the mirror. Not for too long, though. I don't want him upset about waiting on me again.

When I walk out, Jax's face starts to light up. Feels nice to see him smile like that when he's looking at me.

"There she is," interrupting the couple as he pulls me in.

Okay, this feels good. Seen and wanted. Whatever the Lord did back in there, thank you, Jesus, because I was not so sure when we first pulled in.

"Tom and Melissa, this is Alice." We all reach to shake hands. "Tom and Melissa are good friends and former clients of mine."

"Great to meet you," says Melissa. "Have you always gone to this church? I don't think I've seen you before."

"No, I'm pretty fresh to Nashville, actually, but it's been wonderful so far."

"New to Nashville? You and so many others. I swear every weekend we meet a new person who just moved here. Where did you move from?" she asks.

"Well, born and raised in California, but I was in Colorado for a short bit before this too, so kind of all over." Not sure why I felt the need to share Colorado. Slipped right out.

"Wonderful. We love California and especially Colorado. Can't believe you left! Those Rocky Mountains are gorgeous. What brought you here?" Melissa continues.

Stomach drop.

"I mean," I say, pausing for a moment, feeling Jax's eyes looking down on me. "Why not? It's so fun here—"

"Are you ready to head out?" Jax asks me. Even if I wanted to finish the question, he gets us out of there anyway. "Excuse us. We have a brunch reservation to get to. Tom and Melissa, it's been great."

We say our goodbyes, and Jax leads me out of church with his hand in mine. I wasn't expecting public affection so soon, and not after this morning's car ride to church. But even when we get to the car, he opens my door for me, and I feel like I'm back to being on his good side.

"I didn't mean for that to be abrupt. I just can't stand Tom and Melissa," Jax admits as we settle in his car. "They're nosey and can talk your ear off for hours."

"Oh, I didn't think they were a bother. Plus, I want to meet your people, and they obviously adore you. But I am excited about this brunch reservation. I didn't realize you had one planned for us."

"I don't. That's what I'm doing now," Jax says with a minor scoff. "Just had to get us out of there."

I hate that. A little white lie? For what? Just say we're heading out. Who cares if they're nosey and ask a few questions. I was uncomfortable with the "why did you move you here" questions, but now I am even more uncomfortable seeing how natural that lie rolled out of him.

"You're comfortable with a white lie, huh?" I ask, half-joking, half-serious.

"Oh c'mon, I work in real estate. White lies are the name of the game. You're in marketing. You get it, right?"

"No, I don't get it," I say, trying to laugh so it doesn't feel awkward, but Jax is still scrolling for brunch spots on his phone.

Alice, let it go, I tell myself. *You don't know the whole story or their relationship. Let it go. Just enjoy this successful man who picked you to bring to church.*

"All right, this is where we're going. Check it out." Jax shows me a photo of a brunch setting.

"Ooh, mimosas! Yes, count me in!"

"Yes, but nothing too crazy. You don't want to have a bad start to the week. Plus, all your marathon training. You really shouldn't drink too much alcohol."

Another shut down. But I refuse to believe deep down this is the real Jax. No one gets to where he is without being absolutely wonderful. I'm determined to find it in him. I'd like to think I have a knack for seeing the best in people.

*

We're each two mimosas deep, enjoying our overpriced brunch food, and I feel a little giddy. Even Jax has lightened up a bit, and we're having a good time. We're sharing our food with each other, holding hands on the table, and learning more about how he got to where he is now. I'm so blown away by his success.

"Can I ask you something?" Jax looks up at me once the waitress comes to refill our water glasses.

"Do I think you're cute? Yes. How many times do I have to tell you, Jax?"

He laughs and lets the compliment soak in. He loves it.

"Thank you, but no. I'm curious about your move. What exactly does a 'fresh start' mean?" he says, adding air quotes. "Is there something I should know?"

Stomach drop. Again. My body tenses up. Most people accept this answer and move on. They don't see a need to dig deeper. Maybe this is a sign it's different with Jax. An opportunity to show empathy.

"It's sort of a long story," I answer.

"We have time." He's sitting back and looking at me straight on.

I've pulled my hand away from his at this point and started cracking my knuckles, trying to find the right words that won't scare him off. Who knows what he might think of me after this story.

"It was a bad breakup."

"Go on."

"Bad breakup as in 'my engagement ended days before our wedding' kind of breakup."

"You were engaged?"

"Yes."

"So you ended it?"

"No."

"Well, why did he end it?"

"We don't need to go down that road," I push, trying to stop his back-to-back questions.

"Okay," Jax pauses. "When are we going to go down that road? I mean, I think if we are going to be serious at some point, I should know."

This reaction... It's not bad, but it's not good. He has a point that if we date, he should know. However, I'm not feeling as supported in my answer as I hoped a guy would be when I opened up about this chapter in my life.

"Yeah, one day. Maybe just not today."

It's silence between us for a moment, and I can feel the sweat in my palms.

"Okay, my turn," I say, ending the uncomfortable pause. "Why are you still single? You're a catch, Jax. Good looking, established, a man of faith... What am I missing?"

He starts to smile and rubs his hands together.

"Ah, a part of me hates this question, and a part of me loves it. For starters, thanks for reminding me that at *my* age, I am still single, but on the other hand, I love all the compliments."

"So, c'mon, let's hear it. Give me your skeletons in the closet. What is secretly wrong with you that you are hiding?" This question makes him shift in his chair. Maybe my digging is too much now.

"Alice, I don't have any skeletons hiding in any closet." Jax's tone is stern.

"Okay, then tell me why it hasn't worked in the past with other girls."

"Just never felt right."

"Oh c'mon, I'm sure you have had so many options. How could you not find the one."

"I'm serious. This may sound bad, but... Never mind. I'm not going to say it."

"No way, just say it."

"Okay, well, usually I have done the breaking up. Truth is, I don't feel like any girl has been good enough for me. And I know that may sound bad, but I do work hard on myself. My health, my faith, my finances, my career. It felt like every girl I met just saw me as an easy ticket to settle down and get married. Which I want, but I didn't feel like they brought much to the table in exchange for what I was bringing." He looks relieved once the words leave his mouth, but I've lost my appetite.

I swallow and take a second to find the right words. He's waiting for a response, yet I don't know what to say because I don't have anything good to say.

"See? I shouldn't have said anything." He breaks the silence as he reaches his hand over the table again. "I don't want this to change the way you view me."

Except it kind of did.

If he thinks no one is good enough for him, how am I ever to feel good enough? What were these girls even like?

I made a quick mental note to look up what he felt "wasn't good enough" for him.

"No, no, it's fine. I understand that. It makes sense." I'm not believing my own words. "Sorry I asked. I didn't mean for that to take you down memory lane. You're a catch, and I find myself feeling insanely lucky that you saw and picked me."

"You should feel lucky," Jax winks. "I'm kidding, Alice. You're great too. Let's not let those conversations ruin our time together. Are you finished eating?" He asks as his fork makes its way to my plate. Another thing David always did.

What if I don't meet Jax's criteria? When will I fully know before I can avoid another failed ending?

Chapter Thirteen

Birthdays. People either love them or hate them. I love celebrating others, and I used to love celebrating my own just as much. Give me any reason to dress up, put out decorations, and gather people together, and I'm there.

But today's birthday is hard. Because today is David's birthday. Which means mine is in three days. I loved having our birthdays so close. It was an opportunity to really do something grand. One year I flew out to surprise him while we were doing long-distance. I remember having my shuttle driver record a video of me at the Denver airport, where I told him he had about an hour to pull himself together because I was coming to celebrate him. Another year we drove up north and spent the day hiking in the mountains.

That day was maybe my favorite of all of our days together. We had an early morning, which I love. The feeling of coffee running through your veins, driving alongside a sunrise, beating everyone on the road, and groggy morning voices. If I could live in the realm of just early mornings, I would trade it in for late nights.

This day stuck out. Our conversations were fun, the laughter was effortless, and the dreams of the future were promising. The only wedding talk we did was decide on our first dance song. We played it over and over the whole drive home.

Today's birthday celebration is different. New and old emotions are tugging at me. I've been on a path of growth. Dating a new guy who checks all the boxes, new city, new job, new friends, new goals. However, it's David's birthday, and I can't help but think about him. He never was a fan of birthdays, especially his own. David didn't want the big celebrations or having any unnecessary attention, which I always completely ignored.

I wonder if he is doing anything special today. Are people celebrating him? Will he think about me when my birthday rolls around? Does he ever even think about me?

Knock knock.

"Coming in!" Chelsea shouts as she storms into my room.

Quickly, I bat my eyes and lower the music. I don't want Chelsea to think I was crying.

"Why are you listening to these *sad* songs on repeat? Are you okay? I thought Jax was taking you out for an early birthday dinner tonight? Please tell me you're wearing something else." She eyes my full sweatsuit ensemble.

"Okay, wow, first of all, hello to you too. Second, I'm fine. Third, yes, thank you for tracking my schedule once again." She's reminding me that I need to make my way to my closet.

"Sorry. I just didn't want you to be late for Jax."

I don't give her a response as I already feel guilty enough about going out with Jax. After spending more time at Good & Gather with Wes, reflecting on my dates with Jax at therapy, it's clear I should end it. But I can't. I physically can't get myself to bring it up. And to make matters worse, the other day, I let it slip my birthday was coming up, and he insisted on taking me out. The gesture was sweet, so I thought one more shot couldn't hurt.

"Hey, Alice, are you okay?" she says, sensing my purposeful disregard of her comment. "I'm sorry, I didn't mean to barge in, I just—"

"Yes, Chels, I'm fine. Just a bad day, that's all."

"Alice, you can talk to me too, just so you know."

"Sorry, I didn't mean to snap. Today is... Today is a hard day. That's all."

"Is this about the ex?"

"Chelsea—"

"Sorry, it's just that you *never* talk about him, and trust me, I have tried *all* my stalking powers on you to find him and understand what happened. You're so bottled up and secretive when it comes to him."

"Well, it's private."

"But we live together. I see your messes, your hookups, your dirty clothes, dirty dishes. What difference does it make?"

I roll my eyes. Her attempt at reasoning here is pointless. Little does she know I refuse to open up to anyone about it.

"Like I've said, you'll hear about it one day, but definitely not tonight. Now, do you like the blue or pink better?" I'm holding up two dresses for her, unsure why I'm getting her fashion opinion because we have very opposite styles. Hers isn't bad, just different.

"Blue!" she cheerfully says. I note in my mind that I will wear the pink.

"So, what about Wes? Does he know about Jax? I mean, obviously, Wes likes you. I saw how you two were with one another at the shop last weekend. The connection is undeniable."

"No, Wes is just a friend—"

Lies, Alice. Even I don't believe my own words.

"He likes you, and you like him. Why are you wasting time with Jax? Get yourself out of this love triangle."

Ping ping.

Jax: *Wrapping up here. Be there in thirty-seven minutes! You almost ready?*

Jax and his time specificity. Reminds me so much of David. Never late, always punctual, and not very forgiving with people who may run behind schedule. The thought of upsetting him switches me into a different mode.

"Chels, times up. No more questions. I *have* to get ready. Thank you, love you, now bye," I say, gently ushering her out.

I take deep breaths as I look in the mirror. Is it bad that I am going to dinner with another guy on David's birthday?

*

Knock knock.

"Hey, Jax! You look dapper," I hear Chelsea greet Jax at the door. I look down at my phone and see he is two minutes early. Ugh.

"Thank you, Chelsea."

"Alice! Jax is here!"

Using my hand, I fluff my hair a little and touch up my bronzer. I will admit, I look good for only spending thirty-five minutes getting ready. My dress is from Reformation. An early, expensive birthday gift to myself. Spaghetti strap, low V-neck, with a subtle side slip. It's a very hot mini dress, and I'm excited to show it off to Jax.

"Hey!" I walk out and do a little twirl. Jax looks handsome, as per usual, and I can feel his eyes watching me closely.

"Whoa, Alice! You look hot!" Chelsea says, "Like wow, very sexy, very promiscuous. Go get 'em, girl."

"Thanks, Chels." I laugh at her insane compliments, but Jax doesn't respond. He actually looks a little intense. An expression that I, unfortunately, know a little too well, so I walk over and give him a hug.

"All right, you ready?" I ask and squeeze his hand a little tighter.

"Actually, could we talk in your room real quick?"

"Yeah, sure, of course, come on in—" I'm completely caught off guard. Even Chelsea picks up on the vibe change and quickly exits the room.

"You look nice tonight," I say as I shut my door, trying to keep things light and cover the fact that I can feel my heart racing.

"Alice, I don't want to make a big deal of this, but I would like you to change before we go out." Jax doesn't smile. He's not joking. He is serious.

"What? Why? Do you not like my dress? I got it for my birthday—"

"Alice, you look great, trust me. But it's too much. People are going to stare, and I don't think it's appropriate."

"You're kidding. Right? I'm covered up. And so what if people stare? They should stare. I'm walking around next to you, and you're hot. I expect people to stare at us. Now let's go." I pick up my purse again.

"Alice." Jax doesn't budge.

Oh my gosh. He's serious.

"Jax, c'mon. It's just a dress."

"Look, I don't want to seem controlling, but it's too much for a public setting. I'm asking that, out of respect for me, you change your dress."

Out of respect for him? What about me? This can't be real. I thought I moved past controlling men. My diet was straight beans and rice the past two weeks, so I could save and splurge on this dress for my birthday weekend. And he doesn't even have the slightest clue how hard this day has already been for me.

Neither of us says a word as I take a seat on my bed. Jax stands there, hands in his pockets, almost guarding the door. I have a decision to make. I can change the dress, make him happy, and go out tonight. Or I can kick him out and then have to explain this all to Chelsea, Dev, and everyone else who knew I was doing an early celebration with Jax tonight.

Given today is David's birthday, I refuse to be home. My goodness, I can't believe what I am about to do. I know I'm better than this, but I don't want the conflict. Not tonight.

"Okay," I say, letting out a deep breath, "Give me a few minutes. I'll change."

"Thank you, Alice." His body immediately loosens up, and he finally comes over to hug me. "I appreciate it. We should be role models of a sophisticated, mature couple. It means a lot that you understand where I'm coming from."

Oh, Jax, there is so much wrong in that sentence.

"Sure," I say, pulling away. "Hey um, if Chelsea asks, just say that I had a wardrobe malfunction."

"Well, we shouldn't lie."

"Jax, please."

"I'll be outside," he says, ignoring my request. "Thank you again."

How humiliating. I can't even wear what I want on *my* birthday dinner.

Chapter Fourteen

Life has felt off since my birthday dinner. So much so that I stayed in on my actual birthday with Chelsea and avoided the world. No amount of running or online shopping could get me out of this funk. Unsure about what to do next, I made a last-minute appointment with my therapist. These sessions add up, but what happened with Jax set off a lot of triggers for me, and I need a sounding board from someone outside my circle.

After the dinner with Jax, Dev demanded a detailed breakdown and a picture of me in the dress. I pretended to ignore the picture request and only gave her the highlights, leaving out any and all red flags from that night.

Jax is great. I know he is, and I can see it in him. But if I share the truth about the warning signs and moments that set me off, then it would lead to a discussion around David. Which then means I have to open up more about the faulty areas from our relationship. I can't do that. The last thing I want is for her, or anyone else, to see me making the same mistake all over again. Getting back into dating wasn't supposed to be this tough.

As I sit at my desk at work, reviewing my calendar for the day, I see that I totally forgot to block off time for my therapy appointment.

UGH.

Ten minutes until my back-to-back meetings kick off for the day, and there is one particular session blocking my appointment time. But I can't say no to therapy. I need it. My anxiety has been spiked, my emotions are bottled up, and the past couple of days I couldn't sleep.

What is this meeting even for? I click into the invite and read the details. Ah, looks like something I can get by with having just seen the recording. Without asking, I go ahead and change my response to "no" and add a block on my calendar that says "*Appointment—Out of office.*" Hopefully, the word *appointment* makes the last-minute decline more acceptable.

Therapy is great, and it's helped me make strides, but I still feel shame for having to go, which is ridiculous. Everyone should go to therapy, but since I go as a result of the breakup, it feels as if something is deeply wrong with me.

Hopefully, no one needs me on that call. If there are repercussions, I will deal with them later.

*

"So let's go back to the church date," my therapist says. "Tell me more about that."

"It was good. I mean church and brunch. Could a Sunday be more ideal? But I don't know."

She always waits until I speak up.

"I kind of feel like he is too self-absorbed, but I hate claiming that about someone I *hardly* know. This may sound crazy, but I don't think he sees that anything could ever be wrong with him."

"Why do you think he thinks that?"

"He said he was still single because no one has been good enough. I thought he was kidding at first, but he was so serious."

"Why do you think he was serious?"

"Because he didn't flinch. Or even laugh. He looked me dead straight in the eyes. This also followed me sharing my broken engagement. And there was no sign of empathy."

"Sounds a little self-righteous. I can understand why that would be a turn off for you."

"Yes, I mean, obviously, it would be for anyone."

"But it sounds like something that really bothered you. Why is that?"

I wait a minute. Picking at my nails.

"Because it's how I felt with David. I was never good enough. I was never fully what he wanted."

*

The session was productive. Tough, but productive. I could have logged back into work for the day, but I don't think I can get myself to transition my energy and thoughts to marketing. Instead, I decided to go to Good & Gather. Most of the time, I only pop in to write and hang out on Saturdays, but maybe a Thursday surprise will be nice. On my drive here, I got a text from Jax.

Jax: *Hope your day is going well. I just closed on a massive home. Can we celebrate this weekend?*

I think a "congrats" and party popper emoji are enough of a response, but I hold off on sending it. After my chat with my therapist today, it's clear what I need to do, and I don't want to send off any more mixed signals.

As I open the door to the shop, Wes' eyes meet mine right away, and I am greeted with his big smile.

"Well, well, look who it is."

"Hey."

"What are you doing here in the middle of the day?" Wes asks. "Quit your day job to fulfill the dream of being a big-time author?"

"Ha ha, very funny. No, I just took the afternoon off and needed a break from the work chaos."

"Well, happy to have ya. Iced oat milk latte with a splash of vanilla, right?"

"You know it." I'm standing at the counter as he starts on the espresso machine. "So, Wes, question for you."

"Answer for you."

"Do you work here full-time, or do I just have great timing always showing up when you're here?"

"Yeah, I mean, sort of," Wes laughs. "But let's just say you have great timing."

"Sort of? So does that mean you have another job? Or are you living the dream as a full-time barista?"

"Look who came in today with all the questions." Wes looks over at me. "I guess you could say I'm living the dream. Wouldn't trade making oat milk lattes all day for anything else."

"Wait, really?"

"Really. Believe it or not."

"But I mean, do you do anything else on the side?"

"Why do you ask? Full-time barista not good enough for you?"

"No, that's not what I meant. It's just lots of people here in Nashville work one job but chase the dream of music or something bigger."

"Like I said, I'm living out my dream," he says as he hands my drink. "Now I think *you* have some writing to do. I'll check in on you later."

I'm already feeling a thousand times better. I'm so happy I followed my gut and came here to write.

*

Time is flying today. The words are flowing through my fingers faster than ever. Thanks to the help of the therapy session beforehand that helped me get into a headspace where I can write openly and freely about my experience with David, I'm making waves in chapters that were once difficult to write.

"Alice?" My thoughts and typing are halted by a voice. One that I never thought I would hear again.

I slowly turn my body around, and right there in front of me is Adam. David's best friend. Someone who not only knew but allowed David to end things the way he did. The man who David confided in. I also trusted him as one of my good friends. I thought he was a good voice of reason. Until he showed me he wasn't.

After David ended things, I never heard from him. I tried reaching out, but nothing. Not even a "sorry I can't get involved in this, but I wish you well." Nothing. In fact, I'm pretty sure he blocked my number when David did. So why the heck is here and talking to me?

"Adam." It's all I can get myself to say.

"Hey."

"Hi, um... How are you doing?" I shouldn't even be asking him this, but I don't know what else to say. He's just standing in front of me.

"Doing well. Man, I thought that was you when I walked in. Honestly, I wasn't sure if I should come to say hi, but it didn't feel right walking out of here without saying hello." He is so calm, so confident. Acting as if nothing happened.

"Yeah, well, it's me."

"Do you mind if I sit for a minute?" He's already pulling out the chair next to me. All I can do is nod. I have thought about this moment so many times with David, but never imagined I would face the best friend.

"So, how are you? You live here now?" he asks.

"Yeah, I do."

Why are we even doing this?

"And how do you like Nashville?" Adam asks. The audacity right now. How can he sit here and act so calm? He talked on the phone with Dev for hours the night before David ended everything. He knew it was coming, and he continued along his merry way. But when I reached out to him after the breakup asking for support, it was crickets. Not to mention I still haven't heard a word from David.

"I'm—I'm good. Yeah, work is great, very busy, but doing well. And I love Nashville. Probably won't leave any time soon." I feel like an absolute idiot. "What—what about you?"

"Good to hear. I'm doing *really* well."

Oh, good for you, Adam. Love to hear that you're thriving.

He continues. "I actually bought a house out here. Found a great realtor. When you get into a position to buy a home, his name is Jax. I'm blanking on his last name, but he owns his own company. Stand up guy."

The words are piercing through me. He's also a client of Jax's? And what the heck does he mean by "when I get into a position to buy a home?" Screw him.

"What are you working on? Just work?" He points to my computer, which currently shows a document titled "*The Wedding that Never Happened Chapter Outlines.*"

I slam my computer shut. "Just a book."

"Oh wow, a book?" He looks surprised. More so than he did seeing me here. Is he getting joy out of watching how uncomfortable I am right now? "Looks interesting. What's it about?"

"It's um, well… It's a story. An autobiography… Ish."

Pull your confidence together, Alice.

"So a story based on something that happened in your life?"

"Nailed it."

"A recent event in your life?"

"Maybe."

He's nodding slowly, processing my answer, "Alice, look, I don't want to make any assumptions here—"

"Then you shouldn't."

Watching him sit in front of me, acting like he is so innocent. I need to say something. I want to say something, but I don't know where to start on calling out his betrayal.

"I was just going to say—"

"Nothing. You don't need to say anything."

"Alice—"

"No, Adam. You don't need to say anything. You had your chance, and you lost it. Do you have any idea what your friend put me through?" Seeing red, my voice raises, and I can't stop.

"Okay, well, just relax."

"I am relaxed."

"Alice, I'm trying to be cordial here. It took a lot for me to come over and talk to you." He's pointing toward himself like he is some sort of hero. "But if this book is about what I think it's about, please don't do it. David would be crushed."

"David would be crushed? Really? Well, that says a lot since—"

"Alice, stop. Is this a ploy to seek revenge? You should really reconsider before taking a story like this public. You know what people might say or do to David. People would probably think poorly of—"

"Adam, I'm sorry." I hold up my hand to him. "But you have *no* place or right to share your thoughts here."

"C'mon, you and I both know this is not the right thing to do. Everyone needs to heal. I understand that, but airing your dirty laundry? You're better than that."

"Better than that? Stop. I don't need that from you. As if you or your friend have any room to talk about—"

"Look, Alice, I didn't come here to argue. Thought it would be nice to say hi." Adam is scooting his chair back, but I continue.

"What did you think I would say? That it's great to see you? Hope you're doing well? Do you not remember what your friend did to me?"

"I'm not doing this." Adam starts walking away.

"Of course you're not." I yell back at him as he walks toward the door, "First your friend, now you. Always running away from responsibility and confrontation!"

But Adam ignores me and leaves the coffee shop. What is with these men so easily walking away from hard conversations? You started this. At least stay and finish it. Again, I'm left a mess. Not by David, but by someone close to him. Someone I also thought I could trust.

Looking around, I see everyone staring at me. *Oh my gosh, what did I just do?* Wes starts making his way toward me, but this is all too much. Crying. Left alone. Shamed in public. History repeating itself.

"Alice, are you okay?" Wes reaches his hand out, but I push past him and dart for the restroom.

Chapter Fifteen

The door slams shut behind me, and I bring myself to the bathroom sink. Tears won't stop falling. I look high and low for tissues or paper towels. Nothing. Could my timing in here be any worse? Turning to the toilet, I decided to use the last little bit of toilet paper to blow my nose and wipe my tears. As if what happened out there wasn't humiliating enough, I now have to tell Wes to restock toilet paper.

God save me from this moment.

My reflection catches my attention. Have I looked like this all day too? *Great.* Not only am I the crazy ex who just went off on David's best friend, but I also look like an absolute disaster. This isn't fair. Adam caught me off guard. Why couldn't it have been a day after I ran in the morning and took extra time to get ready before coming to the shop?

And why does he live here now? I moved here to escape everything. Everyone. And why does he have to know Jax?

Can this world stop getting so small? This pain is already suffocating enough.

I toss my hair around a bit, but it's not going to make a difference. After every deep breath, I turn to head back out, but the thought of everyone watching what happened sends me back down another spiral. Why can't I stop crying? Needing help, I reach in my back pocket for my phone to text Dev or anyone. Not that she can get here and help, but maybe she can help calm me down.

Of course. Pocket is empty. Left my phone at the table too. My back falls against the wall and I slide down until my bottom hits the ground. Just when I think I was making strides, I'm back to crying on the floor... And in a public freakin' restroom.

Knock knock.

"Busy!" I yell out.

"Alice, it's Wes." Hearing his voice brings me to my feet so fast. Using my hands to fluff my hair in the mirror and my fingers to wipe under my eyes. No, not Wes. Can't he just leave me be? He saw what happened out there. It's embarrassing enough. *Ugh.* Quickly splashing water on my face, I remember, once again, there aren't any paper towels.

Oh gosh, oh gosh. My body is spinning in circles. Do I use my shirt to pat dry my face or reach for the trash where my soggy toilet paper lies? Which is worse at this point?

"Hey, sorry, one minute." Going with the inside of my shirt. *Pull it together, Alice.*

"Alice, can I come in?" Wes knocks again.

"Um... sure." I regret this answer immediately.

"Hey," he says softly. "There she is."

"Hi."

"That was quite the show." His sense of humor, oddly enough, makes me chuckle for a moment.

"Yeah?" I say, letting out a much-needed laugh, "Wait until you see the second act."

"You need anything?"

"No, I'm okay. I just need to get my stuff and go."

"About that—"

"Oh gosh, what?"

"Nothing bad, relax, take a deep breath, Alice." He grabs both my shoulders. "I gathered your things and brought them here for you."

"You didn't have to do that. I can get them just fine. I'm really *okay*."

"Even you don't sound convinced of your own words." He keeps his hands on my shoulders. "Hey, what are you doing the rest of the day?"

"I—I don't know. Hadn't thought that far."

"I want to take you somewhere if you'd let me, of course. I think you'll like it."

"Wes, it's fine. I'm fine. You don't have to do that—"

Wes interrupts, still very calm. "Alice, I can feel you shaking. I know our coffee is strong, but not that strong. I can't let you go back out there like this."

"Wes, I am okay, really—"

"Then look up at me and tell me that," he interrupts. Everything in me tells me to run.

"Okay, maybe you're right." My eyes are still looking in any direction but back at him.

"There we go. When you're ready, I'll be outside waiting. Is there anything else I can get you?" He pushes a stray strand of hair out of my face, which makes me smile and warms my heart. "Maybe some tissues?"

Chills run down my body. Different than the ones from Adam earlier. I finally look up at Wes, and we pause for a moment.

"Is that a no?" Wes reveals that sly smile.

"Sorry, no. I mean, yes." Shaking my head and finally stepping back from his arms. "You're actually out of toilet paper and paper towels in here."

"Dang girl, just using all the toilet paper?" He opens the door behind him. "I'm kidding. I'll take care of it."

The door closes, and I lock it this time. I take another moment to look in the mirror and breathe. My hands still shaking, I play back all the things Adam said and everything I didn't but should have.

Knock knock.

"Hey, it's me again, all clear?"

Opening the door to see Wes standing there with at least eight toilet paper rolls stacked in each hand.

"Delivery!" he jokes.

"What! What are you doing? Why do you have so many rolls?"

"Well, at the rate you were going, I wasn't sure if one roll would suffice." He starts stacking them underneath the sink cabinet. "Plus, hearing you laugh again was worth it. Feeling better?"

"You're a dork, Wes. And yes, I'm okay. Hopefully, I'm not holding up a line of people needing the restroom."

"Ah, no, you're good. I just announced to the shop it's out of order." His attempt at another joke reminds me that people are probably wondering what the heck happened out there.

"Shoot, Wes. I'm sorry. I shouldn't have made such a scene. I really didn't mean—"

"Alice, don't even start. I'm just joking. You're fine. All is well." His arm was holding the door open for me to leave. "C'mon, let's head out. I've been dying for an excuse to leave early, so if anything, thank *you*."

Dipping under Wes's arm, I wait for him to lead the way out. We head out the back door and I follow along until we reach his car.

"Wow, nice car," I say, admiring the clearly new 4Runner. It's lifted, smells new, and feels outdoorsy. But honestly, I'm shocked on a barista's salary, he can afford a car like this.

"Thanks," he says before shutting my door and making his way to the driver's side. "Oh shoot, I forgot my bag. Here, start the car and get the air going. Make yourself comfortable."

Finally, having my phone back, I get ready to text Dev. As I start to type, I think about everything that just happened. No way can I summarize it before Wes gets back. Running into Adam. My public humiliation. Crying on a public bathroom floor. Wes is so comforting. Now I'm sitting in his car. Where is he taking me anyways? I look back down at my texts, and I see the message from Jax still left unanswered. I should respond, but I also don't want to.

"Hey, sorry about that," Wes pops in back. "Ready to go?"

"Where are you taking me?"

"Alice, trust me."

"Wes, I barely know you."

"For now. But I have a feeling that'll change."

*

Although the day has been an absolute rollercoaster, this afternoon could not be more beautiful. The temperature sits at a level of perfection where it's not too hot, not too cold. Wes has the windows down as we cruise through back roads I'm not familiar with, and I let my hair be free in the wind. Wes was right. I needed to get out of there.

"All right, your turn. What song are we listening to next?" Wes hands his phone back to me.

"I didn't think you'd be such a country music fan. I'm going to stick with this playlist you have going. I like it."

"Really? C'mon, I grew up in the South. I can't escape the country music even if I tried."

Okay, his smile gets to me every time. It's so effortlessly warm and cute. Takes everything in me not to pinch his cheek.

"Fair enough. Now can you tell me where you're taking me? We've been on the road for almost half an hour."

"You aren't very patient, are ya?"

"No, I am."

"So you aren't very 'go with the flow' then?"

"What, no. I can totally be spontaneous. I moved out to Nashville on my own. Isn't that 'go with the flow?'"

"Eh, maybe. Why did you move anyways?"

My head turns out the window the moment I hear the question leave his mouth. This time I dug myself into that hole.

"Story for another time," I say, seeing us pull into an empty dirt lot, and that leads to some sort of body of water. "Are we here? Is this it?"

"This is it." He's backing up closer to the water, and I continue to take in the surrounding green trees.

"Wow, this is amazing," I say as Wes reaches for my hand to jump in the trunk of his car. We sit for a moment, taking in the stillness and calming water.

"She's beautiful, isn't she?" Wes says.

Glancing over at him, I see that he is in his element. Relaxed. At ease. Not a care in the world as he looks outward, taking in everything the scene has to offer.

"Thank you, Wes. This really is incredible. I would have never found this place if it weren't for you." A space that lets you be. Where everything gets left behind the moment you look out and accept what nature is offering.

"Hey, thanks for coming along. I haven't been out here for a while. Happy you gave me a reason to come."

"A reason?" I tilt my head at him. "Oh, today! That's right. I'm sorry about that all again. I wasn't expecting to see Adam, and I lost it—"

"Alice, stop apologizing."

"I can't help it. Anyways, that will never happen again. Today was probably my last day ever at the coffee shop."

"What, why? I really hope you don't mean that."

Turning my face in the opposite direction as I feel my face start to blush. I'm shocked he is here with me right now after my whole commotion in the shop.

"I mean it, Alice. I've had this shop for almost two years now, and you are without a doubt the most interesting person to watch."

"What does that mean?"

"You're... You're unintentionally expressive. Yes. That's how I would put it. I don't think you realize your own mannerisms, but they're cute to watch."

"Great, so I'm looking like a fool without realizing it?"

"No, not at all. For example, I can tell when you're stumped on something because you stop typing, slump down about two inches, and look out as you bite your lip," Wes reenacts every action. "The first time I saw it, I'll admit I couldn't help but laugh, but now each time I see you do it, I want to yell out, '*you got this, keep typing.*'"

"So embarrassing." I cover my face with my hand.

"Not at all. Or when you come in, you always take in your surroundings. You're observant and intentional with those around you, smiling at every person you pass by, even if they don't smile back."

"What? No, I don't. That's too much. You're making that up."

"I swear. It's not necessarily a full smile, but you acknowledge people. It's hard to explain, but I see it."

Interesting. Never would have thought Wes pays this much attention to me.

"Well, thank you. I may reconsider my continuation of visits then. To be decided."

"You're welcome," Wes is staying calm and cool.

"Wait. Rewind, you said you own the shop? How did I miss that?"

"You didn't ask." Wes gives me a little nudge.

"I'm *so* sorry. Wait, tell me more! What inspired you to open Good & Gather?"

He pauses. "My dad," he stops again. "My dad was the inspiration. He was, still is, the most incredible man, but he passed away four years ago."

"Wes, I'm sorry, I had no idea. I would never mean to pry—"

"Alice, if you apologize one more time for just being you, I will push you into that lake out there," he says, still managing to be playful. "Don't be sorry. He got sick, and the cancer took him pretty fast. Everything happened so suddenly. Still doesn't feel real most days. But even while he was sick, he still managed to light up every room."

"He sounds amazing."

"He was. He was the type of guy who was always in your corner, and it brought him joy to bring people together. My whole life growing up, he always had gatherings at the house for dinner or drinks. He celebrated others so generously. Everyone loved being around my dad. So when he passed, I quit my corporate job, left the busy life in New York, and decided I would create something here back home that would honor him forever. And so began Good & Gather."

"Wes. Wow." I look at him in awe. "That is incredible. I wish I could've met him, but I can only imagine he is looking over you and is so proud of the man you are."

"Alice, he was. And he was an even better husband. Ah, I would kill for just another day with him."

"I understand that," pausing for a moment. "What would you want to do if you had another day with him? What would you ask him?"

"Hmm. Well, we'd probably get up early. Go for a run, grab coffee, and bring home donuts to the family. My mom loves sweets, and she was the center of his world. And that's probably what I would ask him."

"Which is?"

"The secret to a happy marriage. Love. Finding your person."

My insides are gushing.

"Aw, Wes. How romantic of you."

"Is it romantic? I don't know. But I do know I'll never settle for something less than the way those two looked at each other."

"I hope you find that one day."

Our legs lightly touch one another. Between all the talk and playful nudges, we've naturally moved closer to one another without realizing it.

"All right, Alice," Wes shakes my knee with his hand. "I opened up. Now it's your turn. Let's hear it. I want to know the story behind Alice and what led *her* to visit *my* coffee shop."

"I told you already. Roommate recommendation."

"Stop it. I mean it, what brought you to Nashville?" His voice gets lower. More serious.

"Well, Wes, if you must know," I lightly clear my throat, "Let's just say I moved to Nashville for a fresh start. I wanted something new. I needed somewhere new."

"And?"

"And what?"

"Why a fresh start?"

I let the air blow through my lips. Such a loaded question. Where would do I even begin?

"Mm, rough breakup. Which helps explain the fiasco from earlier."

"Wait, Alice," he jumps out of his trunk and faces me. "Was that your ex in there today?"

"No, thank God. But it was his best friend, who I also used to consider a good friend, but as you can tell, we aren't anymore." I let out a deep breath, "And today was the first time I've seen or spoken to him... Either of them, actually, so it hit a nerve. For obvious reasons."

"Alice, my goodness. I'm so sorry. I wish there was more I could have done to prevent that from escalating today."

"Oh no, you've been great."

"What happened? If you don't mind me asking."

"It's a long story, and..." my chest is tightening up. I don't want to scare Wes off with my past and the truth of what baggage I'm carrying. Or ruin this movie-perfect moment.

"Alice, it's okay, you don't have to tell me. I shouldn't have asked," he interrupts my silence.

"I'm sorry—"

"Alice!"

"What?"

"So help me, I meant it. I will take you down to that lake if you apologize one more time. What are you even apologizing for?"

"I can't help it," I say, smiling as I lightly pat underneath my eyes that started to tear up. Thankfully I am refraining from another emotional scene.

Wes leans forward and grips my knees. "You know what I could *really* go for right now?"

"I don't know, but I have a feeling it's something crazy—"

"A refreshing dip into the lake!" With those words, Wes swoops me into his arms and charges for the water.

"*Wes!* You're crazy!"

He doesn't stop, though. Once we reach a point deep enough, he tosses me out and takes a dive under water himself. Fully clothed, laughing so hard, I don't even notice how cold this fresh lake water feels.

"Wes! I can't believe you just did this. My clothes! My shoes!" I splash water over at him. "You're so lucky I didn't have my phone in my pocket."

Wes swims closer to me, "Eh, it's just material stuff. Here, I'll tell you what, if you're *really* mad about it, and can honestly say you aren't having fun right now, then I will buy you new shoes."

Getting closer to me until we're close enough to see droplets run down each other's faces.

"Okay, fine. Maybe just a *little* bit of fun."

"Hmm, I'm not convinced yet. Admit it, Alice."

I didn't think there was any way we could get closer, but Wes finds it.

"Fine, I admit it. I'm having fun." And with those words, Wes pulls me close to him. My arms wrap around his neck, and his hands on my waist, helping me stay afloat. He's bringing his lips close to mine, and for a second, I'm leaning back into him.

But there's Jax.

"I can't," pulling away, but really wishing I didn't have to. "I'm sorry, there's this guy Jax, and I should clear that up first."

"No, Alice, I'm sorry. I shouldn't have, but I couldn't help it. Which also is not an excuse." Running his fingers through his hair.

Ugh, Wes, don't make this harder. My insides are going crazy. I want to move toward him again. With Wes, everything happened so fast, so naturally.

"Well, he isn't my boyfriend," I say, feeling a need to explain. "But I need to make that clear to him first. It feels like the right thing to do."

"You don't have to explain anything. I understand." Wes gives an assuring smile. "C'mon, let's get out of here."

We make our way back to the shore, and the walk up to the car is silent. My mind is running a hundred miles per hour. Maybe I should have let the kiss happen? Do I really owe anything to Jax? It's only been a few dates. And Wes, while unexpected, is the one I want to be with after this hectic day. But does he think poorly of me for almost kissing him when I have this *situation* with another guy?

"For what's it worth, I had a lot of fun this afternoon." Wes steals me away from my own thoughts. "I do have one request."

"Of course, anything."

"This spot is pretty sacred. *Lowkey* as the cool kids say it." Wes starts taking off his shirt, "Keep it between us, yeah?"

I'm doing my best not to stare at him shirtless. "Yeah, yeah, your secret spot is safe with me."

My gosh, those abs. How do I not look? I turn my head and look back out at the water as Wes rings out his shirt.

"Aren't you going to dry off?" he asks.

"I'm sorry, what? With what? I didn't pack a towel or a change of clothes."

"C'mon, sassy pants. You need to dry off before getting into the car." He reaches in the back seat and tosses something my way. "Here is an extra shirt."

I grab it from the air, and he stands there waiting while I hold the shirt up to my chest. What am I supposed to do with this? Where would I change? But Wes stays standing there, rinsing water off his body and shaking it from his hair.

Shaking my head in disbelief of what I am about to do next, but I don't seem to have any other options. I start to slowly unbutton my blouse, and Wes brings his attention back to me. Normally I would hate this. I would feel insecure about my body and force the person to look away. But I don't. My eyes are on him while I finish unbuttoning my blouse and take it off. Down to my bra, I ring out the water from my blouse and shake out my hair. Wes stands in the same spot. Calm as ever. Neither of us says a word.

"Okay, I think that's enough for today," I say, starting to unbutton my jeans. "Turn around, Wessy boy."

"Alice, you have no idea how beautiful you are." He starts backing up to his car.

I'm fully down to my underwear and a massive t-shirt over my body. The shirt smells like the ground roasted coffee beans from Good & Gather. I could get used to this.

"Ready to go?" Wes asks as I join him in the front seat.

"Yes, I desperately need a shower."

I've never been the girl to strip out of my clothing the first time I hang out with a guy, but here we are. The drive back to the shop is light and easy. Wes is driving shirtless with the windows down, letting the wind blow through his hair.

I can't believe the horrible incident that brought us together here today. If it weren't for seeing Adam and being hit with the painful reminder of what David did to me, I wouldn't be here with Wes.

Without the torment, I would have never had the chance to see what was in front of me all along.

Chapter Sixteen

———

When I get home, I feel like a different woman than when I left the house this morning. Covered in dried-up lake water, uncertain of the contents in my hair, I stand in the shower and let the water rinse away my day. Although a rollercoaster of a day, I feel more like myself. I'm completely exhausted, but I can't wipe this smile off my face. I don't want the day to end.

Standing in front of the mirror, I'm ready to apply self-tanner. I regret not doing this yesterday. Would have been nice to be more prepared when I was half-naked in front of Wes today.

Which reminds me, I need to text Dev.

Me: *Today was insane. Almost kissed Wes. Saw Adam— yes, the Adam. Not in that order, but too tired to type it out. Chat tomorrow?*

Barely setting my phone back on the counter, Dev responds.

Dev: *Adam? What? And you almost kissed Wes? Double what! Wait. What about Jax? Ugh, I hate you for leaving me on cliffhangers...*

Me: *Sorry, but I truly can't keep my eyes open. More to come tomorrow!*

Ping ping. My phone lights up on my nightstand next to me. I should ignore it, but what if it's Wes?

Jax: *Hey you. Hope you had a good day. Haven't heard from you and wanted to check in. Dinner on Saturday?*

Oh, shoot, Jax. Meant to text him back, but I completely forgot. The decision seems clear. No, it is clear, but it's so hard to let someone like Jax go. He checks all the boxes on paper. Good career, good looking, well-established, but after experiencing today with Wes, I see that I was looking for all the wrong things. Once again.

As for a response to Jax: **Sorry, busy day. Let's talk tomorrow.**

That should buy me some time.

*

Thank goodness it's Friday. After yesterday's fiasco followed by the romantic rendezvous, I'm exhausted. Making it through a meeting today without yawning feels nearly impossible.

The phone vibration on my desk perks my attention again. The screen shows Dev's photo.

"Hey, give me a sec," I whisper as I rush out of the office for some privacy.

"Finally! Okay, now dish!" Dev answers the phone cheerfully.

"Hi to you too. I don't have too much time. I have to get back and get a report to my boss by end of day."

"Perfect, start talking, little miss. What happened with Adam? Where did you see him? What did he say? What did you do? Ugh, I wish I could have been there to give him a piece of my mind about him and his stupid friend."

"Okay, calm down. Trust me. I did lose it... You're not going to believe what I did."

Everything I said, everything I did, I recap to Dev. From slamming my laptop shut to yelling at Adam as he left the shop.

"Honestly, Alice, I've been waiting to see this come out of you. Don't feel bad for one second. This is nothing compared to what they actually deserve."

"True, but I still hate that I lost control of my emotions."

"No way. I would even say you didn't lose it enough. Next time throw your drink at him."

"Dev!"

"What? You know they deserve that."

"Okay, maybe. But you know he's going to report back to David. Am I going to be pinned as the psycho ex?"

"No, you are *not* the psycho ex. Do you remember everything he did after the breakup? He is—"

"I know, Dev." Not in a mood to take a trip down painful memory lane, I say, "Let's move on. Want to hear about Wes?"

"Duh! Spill the deets!"

From him coming into the coffee shop bathroom to our drive back home, I don't leave out a single moment. As I replay the story, I can feel myself smiling. I feel good.

"Oh my gosh, Alice. What a dream date."

"No, not a date! I still need to sort stuff with Jax."

"So sort it and date Wes. I want to meet him when I come to visit!"

She's right. I need to sort it, so I start writing out a message to Jax right then.

"Alice? You there?"

"Yes, sorry. Got distracted for a second. Gotta get back to work now. Love you, bye!"

Me: *Hey Jax, can we talk tonight?*

*

The whole drive home I can't get myself to sing along to any music. And for the first time on a Friday afternoon, I wasn't in a rush to leave work. My thinking was that the longer I stayed, the longer I could push back my conversation with Jax. The rest of the car ride is spent practicing what I want to say to Jax.

When I walk in the door of my apartment, Chelsea skips out of the kitchen to greet me.

"You worked later than usual for a Friday," she says. "Any big Friday night plans?"

"I know. I had a few reports to get done by the end of day," I say, rushing to my room. "But I'm going to go for a run."

"Really? But it's Friday night; you always go out on Friday's. And don't you think it's a little late?"

"That's why I'm going now. Need to beat the sunset." I pull the sports bra over my head. My day was stressful. Work was demanding. Plus all the rehearsing of what I was going to say to Jax. And not to mention the uncontrollable gushing over Wes. I need this run more than Chelsea can even begin to understand.

"Hey, before you run off," Chelsea makes her way into my room, "You had flowers delivered here today."

I stop lacing my shoes and look up at her.

"What? Where? From who?" I race past her to search the flowers myself.

"Is now a good time to say I told you so about Wes at Good & Gather?" Chelsea's tone could not be more smug as she leaned up against the wall with her arms crossed.

"You read my card?" I open the already ripped mini envelope to see for myself. These can't possibly be from Wes.

Thought you could use some cheer after yesterday. I hope to see you writing back in the shop again soon. —Wes

"So, what happened yesterday? Is there finally something between you and Wes?"

"It's a long story." I admire the beautiful bouquet before me. Forgot how good it feels to receive flowers.

"And?"

"And I still need to go for that run."

"Alice, come on. I need to know about Wes. Isn't he so great?"

Laughing as I head out the door. "Be back soon!"

The flowers, this gesture. Once again, I am riding all sorts of waves of emotions. I need to talk to Jax before I let anything more happen with Wes. This run was supposed to be a way to calm my nerves, but there is a new adrenaline running through my veins. An extra spring in my step, taking me from nervous to anxious. The sooner I have this talk, the sooner I can go back to Good & Gather and see Wes.

*

When I get back home, Chelsea is thankfully gone. She left a note on the fridge "The tables have turned, and I'm going out with friends tonight. Leftover lasagna up for grabs. Help yourself!" Chelsea really is a great roommate even though we are quite different.

Ping ping.

Jax: ***Hey, any idea on a time when you wanted to talk? Trying to schedule the rest of my evening.***

Then, *ping ping.*

Wes: ***Hey! How was your day?***

I open Wes' message immediately.

Me: *Really fascinating day, actually... You see, I came home to quite the delivery, and I'm curious as to how this random barista knew where I lived?*

Wes: *Ah, but if I reveal my sources, then it takes away the fun.*

Me: *I'll get it out of you one day. But really, Wes, thank you. That was so kind, and you already did so much yesterday.*

Wes: *Of course, Alice. Wish I could have done more. Will I see you at the shop tomorrow?*

Me: *Hmm, I guess I could try and show my face again.*

Still needing to shower, I throw my phone on my bed. As soon as I turn, I hear another text come thru. It's from Jax, again.

Jax: *?*

Shoot. Completely forgot about him in between texting Wes and daydreaming about what I will wear tomorrow. I have to look cute, but not in a way that's trying too hard. Although it hasn't been long, Jax could be more patient.

*

It takes five minutes for me to muster up the courage to call Jax. I'm not going to degrade myself by not talking to him directly, but something in the back of my mind tells me not to see him face to face. It could get ugly. After my trauma with Adam, I don't need another public scene.

"Hey!" Jax answers the phone. "You had me worried. I feel like you have been MIA, and it sounded serious when you asked to talk."

"Yeah, sorry about that." My voice is soft, timid. "Yesterday was a bit of a stressful day, to say the least."

"So, what's up?" Jax snaps back. "What'd you want to talk about?"

"Um," I'm taken back by his tone right now. I thought we would have eased into this topic a little more gently. "Right, well, I wanted to have a conversation about us."

"What do mean 'about us?'"

"Well, the past few weeks have been wonderful. I mean, Jax, you're great. You seem to have it all, but—"

"But what?"

No number of rehearsals for this conversation could have prepared me for his attitude right now. This is never easy or fun, but he is making it harder than it needs to be.

"But I don't feel we should move things any further."

"So you're dumping me?" His voice gets louder.

"Well, Jax, I don't necessarily think of it as dumping. We were never exclusive—"

"Never exclusive? Don't give me that, Alice. My intentions were clear."

"You're right. I understood your intentions, but I think we want different things, and I didn't want it to continue any further if the feelings aren't there for me."

"Wow. Feelings not there? I took you around my places, introduced you to friends and community. I don't get it. If you think I'm so great, then why don't you want to date me?"

Oh, I don't know. Maybe because you're great on paper but controlling and remind me too much of my ex?

"Jax, I'm sorry." Staying as calm as I can, I say, "It's just not going to work."

"You can't even give me an answer? Wow, ok."

"I'm sorry," is all I can muster right now. But I know I shouldn't be apologizing. I have nothing to apologize for.

However, I do want him to calm down. This is way more than I thought it would be.

"So you aren't looking to date *anyone* right now, then? Right?"

Do I have to explain myself to him? Why is he prying so much?

"Look, Jax, I'm sorry. I don't want to waste any more of your time."

"Well, too late for that. I should have known better than to take a chance on you."

"Jax—"

Take a chance on me? As if he was doing me a favor? Now I'm angry.

"No, save it, Alice. You were lucky a guy like me liked a girl like you. It's clear you're trying to work through something. No one moves to a city for a *fresh start* without there being some serious issues behind the story."

Oh my gosh, what is your deal? How rude.

"That's none of your business—"

"You're right, but honestly, I don't want to hear it. I should have known better and taken the warning signs more seriously. You're young and still figuring it out. Good luck to the next guy."

And he hangs up.

Standing in my room, I'm left without words. Frozen. What just happened? Why am I left without an opportunity to voice my feelings? What is it about me that makes men think they have a right to speak to me this way, shut me down, rip me apart with all the things wrong with me?

That conversation went horrible. Falling back on my bed, all too familiar feelings creep back into my body. What did Jax mean by warning signs?

Ping ping.

Wes: *Looking forward to it. Saturdays at Good & Gather wouldn't be the same without you now. Have a good night.*

Hopefully, I am not missing any warning signs with Wes. He makes me feel so good about myself, but is that enough? Could he be another too-good-to-be-true situation?

Chapter Seventeen

———

Feeling defeated from my conversation with Jax last night, I drop face-first on my comforter. Though, it doesn't give me much comfort while tears steam my cheeks and the crushing disappointment balls in my chest. I'm so tired of feeling this way. I hit the pillow and screamed into the mattress. Am I really the problem?

David and Jax shared a lot of similarities, but does Wes have any of those? I'm a little wary now about going to the shop today and continuing this connection with Wes. The more I reflect, the more conflicted I get.

Since the breakup, friends, family, even strangers have told me I deserve better than what David did to me. They're right, but why is it so hard for me to accept that? And believe it for myself?

Noting all the thoughts into my phone, I save it and store the emotions away for the next therapy session. I have to get to the shop and get some writing done if I am going to be serious about this author endeavor of mine. Plus, writing about the pain David caused me will hopefully heal others and bring light to the awful breakup.

*

As I pull up to Good & Gather, I park right in front. It's just the right angle to see Wes wiping down a table near the front window. He looks up at me and smiles.

"Coming in?" he mouths to me as he waves his arm for me to come out of the car.

I put up a finger and mouth back, "one minute."

Both of us are laughing and I watch him turn and head back to the counter. With all the feelings running around in me, I need one more minute to find a sense of calming. Last time I was here, I saw Adam, and that kicked off the best and worst moments of the past several days. Sitting in my car, I read through emails, give Instagram a few more scrolls, and take a few deep breaths.

Everything is okay, Alice. You're okay.

When I open the door to the shop, I'm greeted with a warm hello from another barista. Wes turns around and points to my usual spot.

"Oh my gosh, you guys," I'm surprised to see my drink already waiting for me on the table.

"It was all Wes," the other barista says, looking back at Wes.

Blushing, I turn and head to my spot, hiding the redness I can feel in my cheeks. I was so nervous about coming back here, and already I am swooning over this guy all over again.

"How is your morning?" Wes comes over as soon as I take a sip and open my laptop.

"It's good. Just ran and now I'm writing."

He looks so handsome today. Clean-shaven with a nicely fitted button-down. Not his usual t-shirt and scruff look he typically rocks. Although, he is still as cool as a cucumber.

How does he stay so relaxed? I'm so nervous. I can hardly keep eye contact with him.

"Nice, how was the run? How far did you go?"

"Twelve—"

"Twelve miles? Geez, Alice. What don't you do? Most people are barely waking up, and you've already run more than I have in an entire year."

"Hardly," I say, laughing. "There are lots of people who do more than me."

"Well, I think it's admirable." He pauses and just looks at me. "So when do I get to hear about this book? Tonight?" he asks.

"Um, I don't know." I pause for a moment. "Wait, what's tonight?"

"Well, I was hoping we could hang out. Just as friends, of course, I know you said you had something or someone—"

Waving my hand, I say, "No, no, I don't."

"Oh," he leans back in the chair. "I hope I didn't cause any—"

"No, not at all. It wasn't really anything, but I needed to clear some things up before... Well, some other guy, you know—"

"Some guy, huh?" He puts the words in air quotes. "Well, what about giving that guy another chance to take you on a real date then?"

Looking at him, I want to scream yes. But my insides are questioning if it's too soon. The past two days have included two blow-ups from two different men. Although Wes was the grounding piece throughout the chaos.

"A real date, huh? Not just a dirt road hangout?" I'm trying to tease him while I think about whether or not it's really a good idea.

"Alice, a proper date." Wes sits up and leans closer to me. His tone is serious. He's not messing around.

"Okay." The words leave my mouth faster than my thoughts.

"Okay," he smiles. "I'll pick you up at five. Enjoy your writing. I'll try my best not to distract you."

"Wait," I grab his arm as he gets up to leave. "What are we doing? What do I wear?"

"Hmm," he stops and thinks about it. Clearly he was not planning for an actual date to come out of our conversation. "Something nice. We will do dinner downtown."

"Ooh, fancy. A notch up from the back roads of Nashville."

*

This is nothing I would expect from Wes. The elevator drops us off at a fancy rooftop restaurant that overlooks downtown Nashville. The lights are bright, the view is incredible, and the atmosphere is high-class. Lights are dim, candles on the table, guests are dressed nicely. Even Wes is in a suit. Thank goodness I decided to go with a dress and not jeans.

"Right this way," the hostess says to us as she guides us to our table. I can't help but look around at everyone there. Designer bags on tables, massive engagement rings, and even spot a few red-bottom heels on some of the women sitting at the bar. This does not seem like a place Wes would frequent. I'm shocked.

"This place is stunning, Wes," I say as soon as the hostess leaves our table.

"Yes, that's what I heard. Nicest place in Nashville." Wes is stiff. Clearly uncomfortable. Quite contrary to this morning at the coffee shop. I'm usually the nervous one around him, but for the first time, he can hardly keep eye contact with me.

"You look really nice, by the way. Who knew Weston owned a suit?"

"Weston? Whoa, I haven't heard that in a long time, unless I was getting in trouble as a kid." He keeps his eyes down on the menu.

"Seems fitting for this fancy setting." I'm trying to tease and get anything out of him.

"It's from my old New York days." He looks down at his suit. "I'm grateful it still fit. I should have taken it to get dry cleaned and pressed though. I'm sorry." He shakes his head as if he's actually embarrassed.

"What? Wes, embarrassed for what? Don't be. This is all so wonderful. Really. You did *not* have to do this."

"Well, I wanted it to be more special than the lake."

We pause for a minute while the waiter fills our glasses with a wine that costs more than my hourly wage right now. Which isn't saying much, but I don't think I have ever spent more than twelve dollars on a bottle of wine. I hope Wes doesn't think I need all of this to be impressed.

"Well," I raise my glass up to Wes. "Cheers to a *special* evening."

Clink! Again, Wes is struggling to keep eye contact with me even as we cheer. Something is not right.

"So, how was your day?" Wes asks. "The weather was nice, huh?"

The weather? Really?

"Day was great, and yes, weather was nice." My words are slow as I stare intently at Wes and his body language. "After the coffee shop, I even went and continued to write in a park. It was perfect."

"Good, good," Wes draws out the words like he is trying to kill time. "I think the weather the rest of the week will be good too."

I start laughing and lean forward on the table.

"Wes."

"Yeah?"

"Lighten up! Are you okay?"

"What? I mean, yes, I'm fine. I'm just making conversation."

"About the weather? C'mon, you haven't made a single joke all night or even pointed out something silly about me. I tripped on the sidewalk earlier, and you couldn't have been more silent—"

Even I laughed at myself when that happened.

"Something silly, huh? Kind of like the way you hold your pinky out while sipping wine?"

"*Yes!* Exactly." My voice raises from the excitement of getting a little glimmer of Wes back.

"I'm sorry, Alice. You should know I really like you. And I want tonight to be special after the week you had," he says, as he points his hands around the people sitting in the restaurant, "but all of this, it's not me."

Reaching for his hand on the table, I say, "Wes, I like you too."

"Phew!"

We both let out a laugh that relaxes us.

"And I like you for who you are and how easy it is to be around you."

"You're right, you're right. I'm going to relax now." Wes shakes out his arms and rolls his shoulders back.

"Honestly, Wes, I say we throw this wine back and leave."

"What? But we haven't even ordered—"

"Who cares? We can grab drive-thru somewhere. In fact, I would like to show you my ideal first date. But first, drink up. No wine should go to waste," I give him a wink as I raise my glass with my pinky sticking out more dramatically than before.

"Alice, you're something else. What girl wants to ditch a fancy dinner date for drive-thru?"

"One who knows how to have a good time."

"Let's do it then." And with that, he raises his hand to the waiter to grab our check.

Wes smiles, grabs his glass, and chugs the rest of the wine as he unbuttons the top of his shirt. I can't help but laugh as I slowly watch him sink back into the guy who started stealing my attention when I first went into Good & Gather.

*

"Okay, for someone who runs a lot and cares about her health, you can eat a lot of fries."

"It's called balance," I say as I take a bite.

"So why are we at a Barnes and Noble?" Wes asks. Since leaving the restaurant, driving through Chick-Fil-A, and belting songs from the movie Grease, Wes is back to being the goofy man I knew him to be.

"Before I answer that, I have to say that I can't believe you knew all the words to *Summer Nights*. Who knew you were such a Danny Zuko?"

"I told you this. I did grow up with a sister. I learned a thing here and there."

"Oh, don't put this on your sister, just admit you like it."

"Okay, okay, but only if you're my Sandy. And that secret stays here." He puts his finger up to his mouth, signaling me to be quiet. "Now, can you tell me why you brought us to a Barnes and Noble?"

"Okay, here is the plan. I'm going to set a timer for twenty minutes, and we each have to pick a book for the other person to read."

"Wait, I have no clue what you want to read."

"It doesn't have to be something I would like. It can be a book or topic that *you* like and want to share with me."

"Alice, I still don't even know what kind of book you're writing yourself. What if I am completely off from what you like."

Again with the nerves. Bring back that confidence, Wes.

"That's the beauty! It can be anything, Wes!" There is no hiding my excitement.

"Alice," he sighs and smiles at me. "You are one of a kind."

"I think you'll have more fun than you think," I shake his arm. "You can never go wrong with a new book."

"All right, let's do it." He looks over at me and pauses, then suddenly rips open his door and shouts, "Last one inside has to mop the coffee shop next week." He rushes for the front doors.

"Hey! Wes! Not fair. That is *your* job!" I'm laughing and trailing behind him the best I can in my heels.

Twenty minutes flies by fast. I couldn't decide on one book, so I grabbed two. One about building mental endurance for long-distance running, and another is a sweet rom-com about people who find love in a coffee shop. Felt like the perfect amount of cheesy-ness. After I purchase my books, I turn around and try to find Wes. Time is almost up, where is he?

Searching up and down several aisles, I finally spot him. But to my surprise he is sitting on the ground, leaning up against a shelf, looking down at a book in his hand.

"You know, time is up." I bring myself down to sit next to him. "And I may have not been first in the store, but I think you missing the buzzer qualifies you to mop your *own* shop next week."

But Wes doesn't budge much. He keeps his eyes down on the children's book in his hand.

"Sorry, I just got distracted."

"I see that. Looks like you picked out an interesting book for me to read."

"No, no, I definitely want to pick you out another one." He starts to stand up, and I pull him back down.

"No, tell me about this one. Why'd you pick it?"

"My dad used to read this book to me all the time as a kid." He lets out a deep breath. "It's about a father and son and the crazy adventures they go on together. But it's really just the made-up bedtime stories the dad shares with his son. A story within a story, if you will. He was the best storyteller. He would use different voices and get up and reenact every scene. Just the best dad. Man, I miss him."

Placing my hand on his leg. "Well I can't wait to read it, I'm sure it's wonderful."

"No, we don't have to get it." Wes tries to argue.

"Yes, yes we do. It's perfect."

"Alice, this sporadic date, this kind of night, my dad would have loved it. He was *so* good about living in the moment with my mom and doing spontaneous things. He certainly would never pick a fancy restaurant." Wes pauses a bit before continuing. "I just know my dad would have liked you. I would do anything to talk to him one last time."

"I'm sorry. I can't imagine how hard that is not having him here."

"Sorry I don't say all of this to freak you out, but it's the truth. And something about you makes me want to open up about my experiences."

"Aw, Wes." I lock my arm in with his. "You're doing great. I'm so happy I found someone who embraces my silly ideas. This all so feels good."

"Is this really your dream date?"

"Yes! I can't wait for you to read the books I picked out for you!" I squeeze his arm a little tighter to bring us closer.

"You are such a weirdo," Wes nudges me. "But an adorable one."

"Oh, I'm the weirdo? Do I need to replay the weather discussion at dinner?"

"Hey now, I was nervous."

"You shouldn't be, there is nowhere else I want to be right now."

And right there, in a random aisle of a Barnes and Noble, Wes and I share our first kiss.

Chapter Eighteen

THREE MONTHS LATER

Honkkkkk! Impatient drivers around me are weaving their way in and out of the airport while I sit and wait for Dev. It's been so long, almost a full year, since I've seen her, and I'm anxious for her to experience my life in Nashville.

The past couple of months have been nothing short of magical. After mine and Wes' first date, life is slowly starting to feel whole again. Dev landed in Nashville twenty minutes ago, and I'm trying not to get a ticket by inching my way forward every few minutes.

Ping ping.

Wes: *Hey babe, how's it going? Has she landed yet?*

Me: *Yes! Waiting for her luggage and then I'll bring her by the shop.*

Wes is so excited to meet Dev and keeps reminding me that he has a hundred questions to ask her about me. And not just about me, but he wants to ask her about my family, our hometown, and even crazy college stories. I told him I would tell him anything, but he insists on getting the best friend perspective. It's an odd feeling, having a guy be so invested and genuinely interested in getting to know your people, your past, and every detail that makes me Alice.

Ping ping.

Dev: **Walking out!**

Jumping and screaming, we make the biggest scene. Cars are honking, but we don't care.

"Gah, I can't believe you're here!" I say, squeezing Dev tight.

"I know! Look at you!" Dev pulls back. "Alice, you look so good. I miss you!"

"I've missed you too! C'mon, let's get going before these cars come for us."

"Where are we going first?" Dev asks while we load her luggage in the car, "I could *kill* for a coffee."

"Girl, you know I got you covered on the coffee front."

"*Yes, yes!* Wes' shop?"

"Duh! Would I go anywhere else?"

We spend the next minutes recapping Dev's flight and sharing more details about mine and Wes' relationship. I thought I would be more nervous for them to meet, but his excitement has helped me cool those unnecessary nerves.

*

"Hey! You must be Dev." Wes is already out from behind the counter and reaches out to hug Dev.

"Aww, he is a hugger. I like him already," Dev turns to me and then back to Wes. "Can't believe I'm finally meeting you. I've heard so much."

"Likewise. I'm happy Alice has her best friend here," he says as he pulls me in beside him, "How was the trip in?"

"Easy. Just an early morning."

"Ah, that reminds me; here are your drinks, ladies." He hands us our coffees. He insisted on having her drink prepared before she got here. Oh sweet Wes, turning on the charm. "I need to go help this customer real quick and then I'll come join you."

"Alice! He is such a muffin." Dev says softly as we turn toward my usual spot, "How'd he know my drink?"

"I told him, but only because he insisted on giving you the royal treatment. He knows how much you mean to me."

"So kind! Well, he has my vote already. Plus, have you noticed the way that man looks at you? Now that is a man who has it *bad*."

"What? Not even—"

"Hey! You're back!" Dev says to Wes as he sits next to me.

"No time to waste. I want to hear all about Alice."

"Ooh, like what?" Dev sips her coffee, "Say the word, and I'll dish it."

"Hey now," I interrupt. "Where is your loyalty?"

"Let's start with embarrassing high school stories," Wes continues.

"Yes! Okay, so there was this one time, we were taking pictures before our school's homecoming dance and—"

My face falls into my palms as I listen to the two of them hit it off. We sit and talked for two hours. I knew they would get along, but not this well. My insides slowly shift from excitement to a sense of sourness. This is what I yearned and fought for with David. The lengths I would go to try and get David excited to be around my family and friends. It was like pulling teeth.

And Wes does it willingly. It's effortless. And he likes it. He likes them.

*

"I can't wait to meet your roommate too. She sounds like a hoot." Dev says as we walk up to the apartment door.

"Oh trust me, she is—"

"Hi! You must be Dev. I'm Chelsea, but you can call me Chels. Sometimes Alice calls me that. We are on a nickname basis now." Chelsea is coming in way too hot and hugs Dev. "How are you? It's so great to finally meet someone from Alice's other life!"

"My other life?"

"Oh, you know what I mean. You're just so secretive. So, Dev, do you like Nashville? Isn't it so fab?" Chelsea drills us, well, mostly Dev, with questions as she follows us into my room. "What are you ladies doing tonight?"

"Bartaco, of course," I answer.

"Of course. Where else would you go? Well, if you need something fun to do, you can come join me and my friends at Slam Poetry. It's also Victorian night, so everyone is dressing up." She reaches over to Dev, "Oh and don't worry! I have a few extra wigs if you need one."

Dev shoots me a look that says, "oh, you weren't kidding about her."

"We will keep that in mind, Chels, but I think right now Dev just wants to shower and get out of her airport clothes, right Dev?"

"Right," Dev affirms, "But that sounds very... Interesting."

*

Feels like every person in Nashville had the same idea as us. Bartaco is crowded, the music is loud, the lights are dimming by the minute, and the drinks are endless. I'm not totally drunk, but I am on my way, which is to be expected when Dev and I get together.

"You're right. The margs here are perfect," Dev says.

"I told you!" I hold up my glass. "Found the best marg in the city, great boyfriend, and a new job. It's all coming together."

"Right," Dev puts her drink down. "But besides everything you've done, how are you feeling? I mean, how are you really doing?"

This question feels methodical. Tread lightly with your answer, Alice.

"I'm good, I'm great." I take another long sip. "Life is *so* good."

"You know, you haven't talked about David in a while."

"Well, yeah, no need to."

"Alice, it's me, c'mon. Ever since you moved here, you don't talk about it. I just want to make sure you're okay and taking care of yourself."

"I am. I go to therapy. I do my runs. I'm fine."

The waiter saves me by bringing us our next round. For once, though, Dev stays quiet. She sees right through me without having to say a word.

"Dev, I don't know what to tell you. I'm doing the best I can."

"Alice, I don't want you to think that you aren't allowed to feel sad from time to time, that's all. He was practically your husband, and I don't know. I even find myself wondering about him and thinking about your breakup."

"Don't. It's not your burden to bear. Plus, it's pointless. I haven't heard from him. I thought maybe seeing Adam would trigger him to reach out, but still nothing."

"And nothing about the wedding—"

"Nope." I wave the topic away. "It's fine, though. I handled it all on my own. Plus, you would be the first to know if I ever heard from him."

"What does Wes think about him and that situation?"

"Um," I grab my drink. "He doesn't know the full story."

"What!" She slams her hand on the table. "Alice, you have to tell him."

"Dev, telling someone '*hey, I was once engaged, practically married in fact,*' isn't exactly easy."

"Oh c'mon, every couple shares about their past. You two have been dating for a few months now, and it's never come up?"

"It has, but every time I think I am ready to share, my body physically can't get the words out." My hands cover my stomach. "I don't want to scare him off."

I throw back the rest of my drink and start on the next round the waiter dropped off. Dev is right. I haven't talked about David to anyone outside of therapy and my book for a while. Doesn't mean I haven't endured sleepless nights or gone a day without thinking about him.

"You really believe it would scare him off?"

Sighing as I let my head fall backward against the booth, I say, "No, I don't."

"Then what is blocking you?"

"David." I'm feeling my insides getting worked up. I should know better than to engage in this conversation after drinking so much. "Even after everything, I can't imagine letting him go. He still consumes so much of my mind."

Dev leans into the table, "Alice, I can't speak to the pain and experience you had of a broken engagement."

Don't cry, Alice. Hold it together. It's Girl's Night Out, for crying out loud.

Dev continues. "But I can speak to the incredible woman you are. David, unfortunately, wasn't your person, and I wish you didn't have to learn that in such an ugly way. You've gotta open up your heart, though, and trust that people will understand."

I think back to my book. Why is it so much easier to think about sharing the story with the world and not the very guy I'm falling for?

"You're right, and I know the right person will love me regardless of my past, but what if it isn't Wes, and I'm left disappointed again? Then the '*damaged*' past starts all over again."

"Alice, please. Look at you. It's been over a year, and you have moved to a new state, you're training for a marathon, working at your dream company, and writing a new book. Nothing about you is damaged."

"I guess, but it's not my *dream job*, just a dream company—"

"Stop that!"

"Stop what?" I'm taken back by her snapping.

"All this self-doubt and unwillingness to accept and see your worth. I saw the way Wes looked at you today and how well he treated the both of us. Look, maybe Wes isn't the person you end up with, or maybe he is, but you won't be able to get to that point if you don't first love yourself again. And I am telling you that you are worth the work to get back to that point. That spark is in you. The spirit of Alice we all love and adore. Don't give David or anyone that kind of power to take away who you are and what you have to offer."

Best friends. What would any of us do without them? They love you at your highest and lowest and tell it like it is.

Each word hits me like a pound of bricks. Dev is right. On paper, it looks like I have done everything right to move forward from the breakup, but I haven't taken the time to work within.

Maybe a good first step would be opening up to Wes. After all, my suffering doesn't have to destroy my faith or my future. It should refine it.

Chapter Nineteen

The gravel road is tough this morning. No give, no mercy. Each mile a clear reminder of the late-night girl chats and endless drinks I had with Dev. Her visit was exactly what I needed. Every talk brought me back to center and helped me open up a little more each time. Our conversations helped me realize I need to have this talk with Wes at some point about the breakup and my book.

Today's training run is a long one, twenty miles to be exact, and the best part is I'm not running alone. My heavy breathing is accompanied by the sound of bike wheels spinning next to me.

"You know, we could just turn around right now or stop for a fun break in the woods over there," I turn and joke with Wes.

"Oh yeah? Five miles so far hasn't been enough cardio for you?" He winks at me.

Wes offered to ride his bike alongside me since this was going to be the longest run I've ever done. My body is suffering already, but having Wes by my side makes the miles go by faster.

"Babe, I mean, I'm half-serious." Looking over at him, "You can't take your shirt off looking like that and not expect me to need a little rest stop."

Gosh, Wes is hot. But not like your standard hot. More like the effortless hot guy whose little quirks make him desirable. His longer, curly brown hair blowing around in the wind as he pedals next to me. Sweat lightly dripping down his tattoo sleeve. Dark features that draw you in and give you a sense of protection. Feels like I scored the cool guy and am living out my teenage dream.

"As tempted as I am myself," he says, pulling out an energy gel pack for me. "We came to work today. We can play later." He tosses me the pack to eat.

"Fine," I say, ripping open the pack with my teeth. "So I have a question for you, and let me just say that you don't have to answer now. You can absolutely think about it, and if you think it's a crazy idea, that is okay too. But I just wanted to ask while I had some ounce of courage and since we're out here training together," I pause, taking another bite from the gel pack, "Actually, I don't know, maybe I shouldn't ask—"

"Alice," Wes stops his bike and puts his arm out to slow down my running. "What is it? Just ask me."

"Okay, but really, you can think about it—"

"Alice, say it." He is smiling down at me.

He probably has no inkling what that smile does to me every time. My insides going crazy.

"Okay, okay." I'm catching my breath, "What do you think, or how do you feel about joining me in California for my race? I know it's last minute, but I am happy to help cover flights, and you can save on hotels by staying with us at my sister's, and if it's too soon for us—"

"Alice," Wes gets off his bike and pulls me into him, completely disregarding all the sweat between the two of us. "I thought you would never ask."

"Really? I was so nervous you would think it was too soon."

"I would love nothing more than to watch you destroy your marathon while yelling out 'that's my girl' as you cross the finish line." He reenacts this scene with his hands in the air.

My hands cup his face, and I let the kiss do the talking for how I feel at this very moment.

Pulling back, I say, "Well, and you're committing to meeting my family." I scan his face to see if there is any trace of hesitation.

"Absolutely! Are you kidding me? I can't wait to meet the people who know everything about you. Give me all the baby pictures and embarrassing stories of Alice." He lightly presses his finger to my nose. "I want it all. No secrets. Just pure Alice content in her element with her family."

Right. No secrets.

"Ha, well, be careful what you ask for." I lean over for one more kiss. "Let's get going. Your girl needs to actually finish the race to impress you."

*

Work this week has been slow. If I am not sneaking in personal book writing while on the job, then I'm online shopping. Most of my afternoons are spent at Good & Gather writing and watching Wes work. It never gets old seeing how intentional he is with every customer. The other day I even overheard him offer to help an elderly woman move into a new home.

What kind of breed is he? Gosh, thinking about it makes me anxious to finish out work and see him already.

Ding.

An email comes through on my phone, and chills run up my spine.

Subject line: Congrats! VC Publishing Wants You!

Shut up. No way. Could it be? It has to be! I do everything I can to contain my excitement and not cause a scene at my desk as I read the email from the publishing company.

About a month ago, I submitted my inspirational story to a program that selects twenty authors a year to help get their writing career off the ground. They had asked for a few supporting chapters, but it still felt like a long shot. In my head, I was expecting to have to self-publish, especially with a story as personal as mine. I mean, who cares to hear from a girl without clout like me?

But they did! I want to jump and scream. This is insane. I must text everyone!

Me: ***You will never believe it! Your girl is about to be an author!***

Responses start flooding in from family and friends.

Holli: ***What! Alice, I am so proud of you! I am already dreaming about a book tour for you and what outfits you will wear. You are amazing!***

Dev: ***Shut up! I wish I was back there again to celebrate! Of course, you were selected! Let the world hear your story! You are going to change lives with your comeback story!***

Now to tell Wes. My fingers start flying away like they did with everyone else but suddenly stop. This means I have to open up about everything to Wes. My hands are shaky, and I swear the office just got smaller and hotter. *Relax, Alice. Breathe. Ease into it.*

Me: ***So, I guess all those hours writing at your shop paid off...***

Wes: ***What do you mean? What happened?***

Wes: *Wait! Babe, are you saying you have news about this mysterious book of yours?*

Me: *Yup! I am getting published!*

My phone immediately starts ringing and lights up with a photo of Wes and I.

"*Babe!* You can't give me news like that over a text!" Wes says as I hardly get a hello out, "This is incredible news. Wow, an author? You are incredible. What does this mean now? What's next?"

He has no idea what his support and excitement mean for me right now.

"I know, I know, I'm sorry, I'm still at my desk," I whisper back. "Basically, they need a first draft manuscript in the next six weeks, and I have all these meetings I need to set and deadlines to remember. I just can't believe it."

"I can! Man, I'm so pumped and proud of you." His excitement has only heightened. "Dinner on me tonight. Let me cook for you. I'll bring everything. Don't worry about a single thing. I have it covered."

"Okay, I have a few errands to run after work, but I will let Chelsea know to let you in."

"And Alice—"

"Yes, Wes?"

Pause.

"I—" Another pause. "I'm just really proud of you. I hope you know that."

*

After talking to Wes, I look at the time and see it's still not time to leave. *Gah.* My mind is already done for the day, and I'm anxious to go home and celebrate.

I can hear my boss getting ready to pack up and go, so I decide I will follow suit shortly after. It's a slow day anyway. With my computer still pulled up, I see another email come thru from the organization hosting my race.

Subject line: It's not too late! Run in honor of someone you love.

Hey Runner! We are pleased to announce this year we are partnering with a local Cancer Society to raise and donate funds to cancer research. As a participant this year, you have the chance to dedicate your run to someone. If interested, this is your final reminder to fill the form out here and receive a custom shirt with their name on it. Time and quantity are limited, so be sure to have orders in before 12 a.m. tonight.

See you on the course! Keep training hard!

Oh my gosh, I can't believe I completely disregarded this opportunity with my race until now. Before, I was so hyper-focused on my own reasons for running, but now with Wes going, I should consider this. I think back to the day Wes opened up at the lake about his dad. Or even at the bookstore on our first date. If it weren't for his dad, who knows if Wes would have ever moved back to Nashville?

But would running in honor of him be too much? It's already going to be a hectic weekend with him meeting my family. Maybe I shouldn't add the attention of his dad's passing to the mix. Let me text Dev for a second opinion.

Dev: *Alice, that is so thoughtful of you. 100 percent! If what I know of Wes myself and from what you have shared, I think it would mean a lot. Are you going to tell him beforehand?*

Me: *Mm, probably before we leave, but I will wait a few days. Looks like they'll send me a shirt with his dad's name on it, so I'll wait for that to come first.*

I wish I could go back in time and meet the man who had such a strong impact on Wes. The form is simple to fill out, and I request rush shipping to ensure the shirt arrives on time before I fly out.

Ding ding. The elevator sounds, and I watch my boss head out. Sweet, this is my cue to pack up and go. I hit submit on the form and take a deep breath. What a wild but exciting end to my day. My book, Wes, the race dedication. It's all coming together.

On my way down to the parking lot, I text Wes.

Me: *Leaving now. Be home in about forty-five. I can't wait to kiss you!*

Wes: *Perfect! Just got here. Ready to celebrate my author!*

Chapter Twenty

———

"There she is!" Wes cheers and rushes to the door. Before I can even set my stuff down, I'm lifted and swung around in the air. My absolute favorite feeling.

"Ah, babe!" I yell out.

"I can't help it," he sets me down and gives me a long, much-anticipated kiss since I shared the book news earlier this afternoon.

"Okay, we get it: you're in love," Chelsea chimes in, standing right next to us, signaling that we need to stop all the kissing. "Wes shared the news. Congrats, roomie!" she says while also embracing me for a hug.

"Thank you, both of you! I'm so thankful I can come home to people who want to celebrate with me."

"Speaking of, here is your wine as promised." Wes hands me a glass.

"Aww, thank you. All of this," I say, pointing at the food in the kitchen ready to be prepared and the beautiful flowers on the counter, "you didn't have to."

"My girlfriend is an author. Are you kidding me? I'm the lucky one who should be thankful." Wes continues prepping dinner.

"You two are adorable," Chelsea interrupts our gushy exchange. "And I wish I could stay and celebrate, but I myself have a date."

"Oh my gosh, wait, what? Really? With who?" I ask shockingly, to which Wes fires me a look that says "*easy there.*"

"Well, don't sound *so* surprised," Chelsea says, "And you can actually thank your boyfriend, he introduced me to him at Good & Gather the other day."

"Well, would you look at that." I look over at Wes, who brushes off his shoulders. "Who knew so much love could be found at Wes' shop?"

"My coffee has that effect on people," Wes teases back.

"Okay, Chels, spill. Give me some deets before you go."

"Yes. So this guy, he was sitting all alone and reading a comic book, which normally I wouldn't be too fond of, but then I overheard him on a call talking about how he volunteers at the local dog shelter. He is so cute, Alice. So, I got up and asked Wes if he knew him. Then before I knew it, Wes came over and played matchmaker. It was perfect."

"Well, would you look at that." I nod at Wes. "He sounds great."

"He really is a good guy," Wes chimes in. "I've seen him in the shop a few times, and he's always friendly. And he tips our baristas well, which I appreciate."

"So kind. I love that," I say, looking back at Chelsea.

"All right, well, I'm off. And don't worry, Alice, I'm not you. Two hours max, and I'll be home," Chelsea turns and heads for the door. Wes and I both laugh as she leaves. It's the unnecessary little banter from her that makes her so unique.

I turn to go change and get settled when my body gets swooped up by Wes again.

"I thought she would never leave," Wes says, and before I can even protest, he starts heading toward my room.

"Wes! What about dinner? You better not set my kitchen on fire!"

"Trust me, will ya?" Wes kisses me and continues down the hall. "We have to celebrate the proper way now."

Wes pushes my door open with his foot, still keeping me securely held up in his arms. He gently lays me down onto my bed and turns around to go close the door. As I lie there, I kick off my shoes and start to scoot back and get comfortable. I'm about to tell him not to worry about the door until I turn and notice my laptop is open.

Wait a minute. I know I can be in a rush some mornings, but I never, *ever* leave my laptop open. When it comes to my computer, I keep it closed and put away. So why is it out and open? I roll over and hop off my bed to my desk.

Did Chelsea go through my room?

"What are you doing? Get back here," Wes tries to tease and pull my arm back toward him.

"Sorry, I just... My laptop is open, why is it—" And before I can finish my sentence, I see it's open to a chapter of my book. This is no accident. It was obviously Chelsea. Gosh, I let her use my computer one time, and now she has gone too far.

"Ugh!" I let out. "What an absolute invasion of privacy. I let her use my computer once, and she thinks she has right to it. She is always in my space, but this is too much. This wasn't for her to—"

"Babe, calm down. What's wrong?" Wes asks.

"Chelsea. That's what is wrong," I slam my laptop shut. "She's always been a little nosy, and I wrote it off, but she—she went through my book. She read it without my permission. Who has the audacity to just invade privacy like that?"

"Well, does it matter?" Wes questions. "I mean, if you're going to publish it now, everyone will eventually read it, right?"

"Yes, but not until it's finished, and I've actually come to terms with it being ready for the world to read. But she knows I'm private about it, and she's always asking questions. I can't believe she went behind my back like that—"

"Alice," Wes calmly interrupts.

"What?" I snap and realize he isn't the person I need to be mad at. "I'm sorry, I don't mean to take it out on you."

Wes comes closer to me, "Alice, you can't keep hiding your breakup like this—"

Hold up.

"Wait, my what?" I look at him standing before me. "Wes, please tell me *you* didn't snoop on my laptop."

"Babe, it wasn't snooping—"

"Okay, no. First of all, you don't get to *'babe'* me right now." My hands cross as I create further distance between us. "Secondly, why would you just go through my stuff without my consent? What gives you that right? That is my property."

"I'm sorry," Wes reaches for me to come closer. "I thought that since it's getting published, it would be okay. And I didn't mean to go looking for it. I was looking up a recipe and saw the tab open—"

"No. There is no excuse here. My stuff is not your stuff. And that story..." Emotions flood over me. "That story is *mine*. It's mine to share when I'm ready."

"Alice—"

"No, you took that decision away from me. You weren't supposed to decide when I share it with you, I was."

"I'm sorry."

"You just have no idea, Wes. No idea how *little* control I had over the breakup. This book is the one thing I was able to control. It was... It was horrible, and you just went into my space like it was nothing." Tears fill my eyes.

"Alice," Wes pauses while I try to gather myself. His hands are holding my arms tight at this point. "I'm only going to ask this because I care."

"What?"

"Are you even sure you're ready to share this story with the world?"

"Stop." I move myself back away from him again. "How could you even ask that? How much did you even read?"

"Enough to know that this book is about to reveal every little detail about your former relationship." Now he sounds a little bothered by this conversation.

But we both pause. We both know there is more to that statement than him just stating the obvious. Something in the air tells me he has more to say. It's the kind of pause you experience before you are about to be told something you don't want to hear.

Unfortunately, it's a feeling all too familiar.

"What, Wes?" I say, breaking the silence. "Just say it."

"Alice." He tries to close the gap between us again, but I'm not having it. "You know I care deeply about you and only want what's best for you—"

"Oh, cut the crap, Wes, I'm not a child. I'm a grown woman. Don't try to soften a blow. Say what you feel so inclined to say."

"Alice, I don't think you're a child," he says defensively. "I do, however, think you are a respectable woman, and I, for one, respect and admire you so much."

"Oh my gosh, Wes, what?" My patience is growing thin. Although, I don't know why I am even giving him this much space to talk after what he has done.

"Look, I understand I don't know the full story—"

"Exactly, you don't know anything."

"Well, that's because you run or change the subject any time it's brought up, and honestly, I don't think writing a tell-all book about your ex-fiancé is the right thing to do. Look, I wasn't going to say anything because I am so proud of you for getting selected for publishing, but since you asked, you're right. I don't think this is the best idea for you, at least not in *that* style."

Back to square one. We are back to square one. No, I am back to square one. Another man who thinks he knows what is best for me. I'm not doing this again, and I certainly won't stand here and beg for him as I have in the past. After the work I have put in for myself to regain strength and my self-worth, I won't let Wes take that away.

"Get out," I say as calmly as I possibly can.

"What?" He seems confused and bothered. "Why?"

"Because you broke my trust, invaded my privacy, and now you're trying to push your own feelings onto me."

"Alice, no, you are misunderstanding me. Please let me explain. I'm not opposed to you writing about your experience, but that, what I read... It's just not the Alice I see and know."

"Well, maybe you don't really know me." I pause for a moment. "And you certainly don't know my story the way I do."

"I don't," he sounds defeated. "You're absolutely right."

We both stand there for a moment, and I refuse to look up at him. I can feel him waiting for my next words, but I'm overwhelmed and feeling disappointed in myself. Finally, I see him turn around and head for the door.

"Alice, for what it's worth, I hope you know I only have the best intentions for you."

As he leaves, my body falls to the ground. Curled into a ball, I let the tears fall. An all too familiar pain of heartache raging through my flesh as I watch a man who I deeply care for let me down. After David, I didn't think it would be possible to love someone again. But with Wes, it came so easy. And now I am crumbled, defeated.

Wes didn't have his future stripped from him. I did.

Wes didn't have to purge all of his belongings because every single thing he owned held sentimental value. I did.

Wes didn't have to bare the shame and embarrassment. I did.

Wes didn't have to pull his stuff out of a storage unit. I did.

Wes didn't get told he wasn't worth spending the rest of his life with. I did. He can have the best intentions for me, anyone can, but that doesn't erase what I had to endure.

Chapter Twenty-One

The crisp beach air makes this morning's run a breeze. After flying into California late last night, my body, still living in another time zone, woke me up early. However, I didn't fight the wakeup call. Instead, I took it as a chance to get my last taper run in before my race this weekend.

And to clear my mind before everyone else wakes up.

Can't believe I'm here without Wes, and we haven't talked in over a week. The last I heard from him was a voicemail he left confirming he wouldn't be joining me in California to honor the space I need, but he wanted to wish me luck.

But do I want space? I miss him.

Wes read my story, and he still wanted to congratulate me on my success that night. He still wanted me after knowing I had a horrible breakup. But he also invaded that sensitive space of mine. He'd taken away the time I needed to prepare myself for telling him my story. That intimate piece of my life I've been working through.

Ugh. Why is it that I was so ready and willing to share my story with the world but not with Wes? Why am I still allowing myself to sit in shame and embarrassment… Especially with the people who care for me the most?

I can't keep running away.

As I come up to the beach, I spot an empty bench overlooking the water. The tide is high, and the sound of the waves crashing helps me relax as I find a breathing pattern to cool my anxiety. My thoughts have been running wild this morning.

Santa Barbara, the beach, the coastal air, it reminds me of mine and David's trip here once. This was the place he told me he loved me. I thought he was crazy. We hadn't even been dating that long, but when he said it, I was his forever. From that point on, he knew he had me wrapped around his finger. That I would go to the ends of the earth for him, even knowing he wouldn't for me.

And now here I am, single again. But this time, I pushed someone away. The irony makes me laugh at myself. When I think about it all, I don't even recognize the girl I was with David.

If David were here, what would he say? Would he have anything left to say? What would I say to him?

With the wide-open space in front of me, I let the sounds of nature calm me in this time of reflection. My heart feels a tug to write. I'm not sure what exactly, but there is an undeniable calling in my chest to let the words flow out and bring them to life. I know what I need to do if I ever want to move forward with someone else. I have to let go.

My thumbs start to fire away as soon as I open up the notes app on my phone.

Dear David...

*

"How are you feeling? Ready for your race?" my dad asks as I join him and my mom on the back patio for morning coffee.

"Ready as I'll ever be," I say, curling up next to my dad. "There's no going back now."

"Nervous at all?"

"Mm, just anxious to finish it," I say, sipping my coffee.

"Between the race and your book news, you are having quite the success!" my mom shares.

"Yeah, I guess so."

"Why don't you seem very happy about it?" my mom asks.

"No, I am—"

"What is it?" mom continues. "Is everything okay?"

"I don't know. It all reminds me of the reason why Wes isn't here this weekend."

"We were curious what happened," my dad says. "But you're dealing with so much we didn't want to pry."

"He read parts of my book. Without my permission."

"Well, won't everyone read it at some point?" my dad looks at me, confused.

"Yes, but on my terms."

It's clear that the wheels are turning in my parent's head as to why I'm so protective of the story if I'm about to share it with the world. Since it's based on my life, I want my book to be received well. And I want it to be a story that empowers people to own their stories.

"What do you want, Alice?" asks my mom.

What do I want? Struggling to answer the question of what I want, I think about what I don't want. Deep down, I truly don't want David to ever feel what I felt. I don't want revenge. People can say what they want, but I loved him. What I want is peace with myself, peace with the breakup, and acceptance that I can't change the past.

"I want to move forward. I want to inspire others." I pause for a moment. "And right now, I really want Wes."

For the first time since David left me, my parents and I have an honest and open conversation. The walls come down, and my emotions flood out. Everything from what I failed to see in my relationship with David to areas where things went wrong. The times I should have spoken and stood up to him to realize my worth.

Naturally, tears fall. But my spirits are lifted. Whether it's Wes or not, I need to learn to trust myself and those I choose to be in my life. I can't continue living life trying to run from my past yet letting it stop my future.

"Alice, if there is anything I hope you know and fight to understand, it's your own worth," my mom shares, "You are worthy of being sought after and fought for. Life isn't always easy; relationships take work, but you, Alice, you deserve someone who would do anything to be with you."

"Thank you," I say, wiping my eye. "I'm sorry, I didn't mean for this to get so emotional. It's just that moving forward with Wes has really opened my eyes."

"Wes sounds incredible," my mom says. "I really wish we could have met him."

"Me too. And now you probably won't. I pushed him away, I just know it."

Chapter Twenty-Two

––––––

A few sips of black coffee is enough to wake me up, but not too much to send me running for the bathroom mid-race. Half of a banana. Phone fully charged. Watch charged. Headphones charged. Spotify playlist long enough to get me through the race, with a few songs specially picked by people I love so I can think about them as I run. An outfit thoughtfully put together. Hat to prevent sweat from dripping into my eyes. Electrolytes in one bottle, water in another. My most cushioned socks and cute race day sneakers to feel my best for the next 26.2 miles.

It's race day.

Thankfully it's still dark out, which I love. The less I run in the sun, the better because it's draining, and I need to conserve as much energy as I possibly can.

"Good luck," my mom gives me a hug. "Your dad and I will do our best to catch you throughout the race and at different mile markers."

"You got this," my dad says next. "Not a doubt in my mind you won't crush this race too."

I'm so thankful my parents got up early with me this morning. Helps get the adrenaline going knowing I have them here to watch and support me. And I'm doing my best not to focus on the fact Wes isn't here. After the talk I had with my parents, I wish I could tell Wes everything

I'm feeling. While it may appear to people that I've moved on from David and the breakup, the truth is, there is still a lot bottled up.

Wes is the first person who has really challenged me to open up. And I want to open up. I want to make those changes. My only hope is that it's not too late.

Shaking off the thoughts and nerves in between each stretch, I breathe in the energy of the runners around me. Watching as people kiss goodbye to their partners before jumping in the corral with the rest of us. I want that.

"Good morning runners, we are starting the sixty-second countdown. *Who is ready?*" the announcer exclaims over the loudspeaker. People around me start cheering, clapping, and running in place. The reality of this race really starts to set in as I watch the clock countdown.

Deep breath. Deep breath. You have trained for this, Alice. You got it.

The horn goes off, and we all start moving forward.

*

Four miles in, and my pace is perfect. Feeling better than I planned. People running alongside me have the most contagious, positive spirit. "*You got this! Keep going!*" are cheers shared from both spectators and competitors. What a neat experience to feel everyone supporting one another as we embark on this lofty goal. We are just as crazy as the person next to us to sign up for this, and each of us has our own reason for accomplishing this run today.

Buzz buzz.

I feel my watch vibrate, but I ignore it. Probably just the family group chat, although it is fairly early for conversations.

Buzz buzz. Okay, what could my family possibly be talking about this early? It's still 5:30 a.m. I look down and see Chelsea's name pop up, and her texts keep coming in. What does she want? She knows I'm running today. Looks like several messages, but it's not until I see one particular name that guts me.

Wes.

Chelsea: **Hey roomie, so I know you're running, and I wanted to keep this a surprise. But then I panicked you might hate me if I didn't warn you...**

Chelsea: **I'll just say it... Wes is coming to you.**

Chelsea: **Well, he's probably already there.**

What! *Deep breath. Okay, keep running, Alice. You can't let this stop you.*

What does she mean Wes is here? Just in California or at the race? Why would he come now? He already told me he wasn't, and we haven't talked. What did Chelsea say to him? Why does she, of all people, know he is coming? Oh gosh, I haven't even practiced or prepared what I want to say to him. I'm not ready for this.

"Hey, Alice! Looking good!" the all-too-familiar voice hits me. Looking ahead, I see Wes waving his hand with that stupidly charming smile of his.

You have got to be kidding me. How? Why?

"Wes?" I yell out to him as I start weaving through runners to get to the sideline.

"Hey you," Wes says so calmly.

"What... What are—" I'm completely out of breath.

"Alice, why are you stopping?" Wes lightly laughs. "C'mon, you have a race to finish, don't stop for me."

He is trying to make light of this moment, but all I can do is hug him. Squeezing him so tight and letting my head rest on his chest, I finally pull away. I notice the shirt on him. The front says, "*Today I run for those who can't*," and the back has his dad's name across it. But how did he get this?

"Wes, what are you? Why are you?" looking him up and down in complete disbelief, "This shirt... You look—"

"Like a guy who is so madly in love," he cuts me off. "Look, Alice, we can talk later, but I couldn't imagine missing this moment. And this shirt reminded me of your heart, your spirit, and your drive. Alice, I am so in love with you, and I would be crazy not to be here for you."

Pinch me. This can't be real.

"Wes, I love you too." I look back up at him. "And I'm so sorry—"

"I know, I know. Me too, Alice." He pulls me in for another quick embrace. "Here, I think this shirt looks better on you."

He pulls out another shirt from his backpack to replace the one I ordered to dedicate to his dad.

"I can't believe you put this on. You look so silly," I tease as I watch him change right in front of me and everyone around us.

"Alice, you have no idea how crazy I am about you. I never want to go another day without talking to you."

He hands me the shirt, and I start ripping off my current top. Slightly embarrassed, I hand him back my sweaty shirt.

"Ooh, now this is my kind of run! I like the shirt, but I love this wardrobe change more," Wes jokes as I give him a playful punch. "Oh! By the way, your dad told me to tell you he has extra energy gel packs at mile seven for you."

"Hold up," I pull the shirt over my head. "You already met my parents? How?"

"Don't worry about it, rockstar. Now go kick butt. See you at mile seven." He slaps my bottom and takes off running as if he has somewhere to be.

What just happened? How did he get here? I thought he canceled his flight? Where did he stay? My mind has about fifty unanswered questions, and at the same time, my adrenaline is higher than ever. As if I wasn't already feeling good about my run, I feel unstoppable now.

Wes came. He is here. And he is here for me. And he loves me. He didn't just say it. He showed it.

*

After stopping at mile seven, I'm starting to uncover why Wes was in such a hurry to run away from me. Since then, I've been surprised with a new person at each mile marker. Mile seven was my brother Mitchell and his wife Kim, then mile eight were my sisters, JA and Lizzie, and mile nine was Holli. The list of surprises and people go on. From family to friends, I'm speechless at the support of everyone who has shown up. Especially this early. The sun is barely rising.

"You're nuts! I can't believe you're here. It's so early!" I say to my brother William at mile ten.

"Of course I am! We all are. Keep running!" he cheers back to me.

With each mile, I am reminded of what love and commitment not only look like but feel like.

Mile twenty-three comes up, and it's a monster of a hill. My legs are heavy and ready to give out. People say after mile twenty, it's a mental game to get to the finish line, and I fully understand that game now. Wes told me at mile twenty-two he would see me at the finish line, so these last three miles are left to me to conquer on my own.

Overwhelmed by the excitement and adrenaline of this race, I can't help but feel emotional. I have the support I need, and I know I won't be alone in the end. But now, it's up to me to prove to myself I can do this and cross the finish line. Similar to the past, the breakup, the shame I have felt, I can decide if I am going to let this hill own me or if I am going to own it.

The climb is worth it. Where there is pain, there is growth.

*

Finish line around the corner! Keep going!

I have never loved reading a sign more in my life than this one. 26.2 miles is no joke. And I am not just excited to be done running, but I am eager to hug and see all my people together.

Especially Wes.

As I turn the corner and the finish line comes in sight, so does my tribe. My friends and family. All awake bright and early, holding signs, cheering out my name with smiles so infectious. Giving them a strong finish, I sprint through to the end.

"You did it!" I am immediately swept up into the arms of Wes.

No runner's high could ever compare to this moment. Completely unapologetic of how sweaty I am, my arms and legs wrap around him.

"Thank you," I whisper into his ear.

"I am so proud of you, Alice," he whispers back, and I watch as everyone comes up to join us.

He lets me down, and I'm flooded with hugs and smiles from everyone else.

"I can't believe all of you are here," I say, wiping away my sweaty, happy tears. "This... This is so special. You didn't have to do this."

"Wes planned it!" Holli says. "He reached out and made sure all of us secured this weekend to be here even before you decided to invite him."

"Yeah, it was all his idea," Dev continues.

"Wait, you did this before I even invited you? How? Why?" I pull him closer to my side.

"Because you were working so hard, and you deserve to be celebrated and loved whether it's by me or not."

"Yup, he covered and planned everything. We are so happy he still came out. He is just as wonderful in person as he is over the phone," my mom says.

"He really is wonderful," I say, giving him a quick kiss. "All right, now can we *please* go get brunch? And a shower!"

All of us gather together for photos before leaving the race site. This is one of those I don't want it to end moments. Every hug, every smile, every person here has helped me through thick and thin. They accepted me at my lowest, and now we're celebrating me at my highest. This is it. This is what love is. I grab Wes' hand and let him lead me to the car.

"Okay, mister, now that I have you alone, you have some explaining to do. How did you pull this off?"

"Alice," Wes starts laughing, "Just let me surprise you and take care of you."

"But I mean, all of my family, my friends, how?"

"Look, I hope never to stop surprising you the same way you never cease to amaze me. Enjoy this day and your moment," he squeezes my hand a little tighter, "Oh and Alice—"

"Yes?"

"Thank you."

"For what?"

"The dedication. Thinking about my dad when this race was meant to be about you. I've said it before, but I want to say again. He would have loved you."

"Wes, you don't have to—"

"Alice, please, let me," he interrupts and stops us before even reaching the car. "He would have loved your family, this day, everything. The other day I couldn't take it anymore, so I went by your apartment to apologize and make things right, but Chelsea told me you decided to come out to California a little earlier. That's when she showed me the shirt and mentioned the race dedication."

"For once, I'm thankful for her being nosy."

"Me too. You should have seen how fast I ran out of that apartment and booked the flight to come out here. So thank you again for doing this for me and my dad."

"Wes, I love you, and that means everyone and everything that comes with you."

"Good, because I am never letting you go again," he kisses my forehead, "Now let's go get you some mimosas!"

Chapter Twenty-Three

___

After the race, Wes suggested we extend our trip in California to spend more time with family and friends. He wanted more time with everyone, and quite frankly, I was eating it up watching him. Wes charms a room without even trying. His natural curiosity to learn about someone helps him engage with people so effortlessly. Over the past couple of days, I observed him play countless games of soccer with my nephews, help my mom cook dinner, and even join my dad on the golf course. It's one thing to be loved and accepted by someone, but it's a whole other level of love I didn't know could exist when you see that same person love and accept all the people in your life.

It was no secret they all loved him too. Any chance someone got a minute of alone time with me, they expressed how impressed they were by him.

I believe JA's exact words were, "Now this is the man I have prayed would find you."

The thought of bringing someone new home after David made me nervous. I feared the comparisons that might be made, but there hasn't been a single afterthought or mention of David. Almost as if everyone in my life has a mutual understanding that the David phase is over.

Doesn't mean that chapter will ever be forgotten, but it feels like everyone is ready to move forward with me.

＊

The night before leaving, I finally get some alone time with Wes outside on the back patio.

"Well, everyone loves you," I say, snuggling up next to him with my glass of wine.

"And I love everyone. You have a great family, Alice, and I am so happy to be here," Wes squeezes my leg. "I think our families will blend together so well."

"I think so too. Your mom is pretty great. I totally see her and my mom hitting it off. Just the purest, sweetest moms on the planet."

"Oh, for sure. We will get them together when your parents come out to visit Nashville. I always wanted a big family. Imagined it being so much fun. Your family has proven that thought to be true."

We relax there for a moment. With a family as large as mine, the noise is constantly loud. I can only imagine Wes needing this quiet break as much as I do.

"So, we still haven't talked about the book," I lightly change the subject, but it feels necessary to do before we head back.

"Alice, look, it's your story, not mine. You were right—"

"No, Wes, let me talk, please," I say, interrupting him. "I'm not publishing it."

"What? Why?" He pulls himself up. "Please don't let my own emotions get in the way."

"No, they didn't." I look back at him, "Okay, so they sort of did, but not in the way you're maybe thinking. What happened with David was difficult. It was, and still is, the kind of pain I wouldn't wish upon a single person."

"And I wish there was something I could do to take that pain away from you."

"Thank you, Wes, but I'm serious here. Deep down, what I really want the book to achieve won't get done if I go about it the way that first copy was written. So I'm declining the offer."

"Alice, are you crazy?"

"Hey now," I say, joking with him. "Tread lightly, Wes."

"Sorry, it's just that you said writing a book was a dream of yours—"

"And it still is."

"So why are you giving up when you're *so* close?"

"I'm not. I'm going to rewrite the book. One that is focused on where I am headed, not where I was."

"Okay. Tell me more."

"I want to inspire. I want to make an impact. I don't want to feel people's pity. My hope is that they hear my story and know they, too, will be okay. Writing a tell-all book is not something I will actually feel good about in a few years."

"Wow. Well, I commend you for being willing to start over. That can't be easy."

"I mean, it's not my first time starting over." Flipping my hair, I say, "Look at me now."

"You're a dork," Wes laughs.

"And you like it."

"Can't deny that. Well, Alice, whatever you write and set out to do will be amazing. I'm so sorry you were hurt so badly, but I am so immensely proud of you for finding and owning your strength. You're going to make a difference in others' lives, and I know this because you have already made one in mine."

"Wes, so sweet. You're going to make me cry again."

"No, no, no more crying," he says, cuddling me a little closer.

"Okay. So I do have one little request."

"Anything." He's running his fingers through my hair. "You name it."

"Our layover is in Colorado. And I want to stop there for a day. Is that okay?"

"Absolutely. Are you sure you want me there? If you need space for that—"

"No, I want you with me. Always."

"Then I will be there. Always."

*

The flight into Colorado is oddly okay. I'm anxious to make peace with this place but also thankful to have Wes. We cuddled the whole two-hour flight, and now holding his hand as he carries my bag through the terminal makes me feel so secure. Especially in a place where I thought that feeling would never be possible again.

We grab a rental car and head toward Colorado Springs. Our layover is long, and we've been up since the crack of dawn, but Wes is doing a great job keeping spirits high as we head into a really emotional space.

Last time I was here I didn't leave the way I would have liked. Scatter brained, confused, and still in shock from what happened. And not even just *what* happened, but *how* it happened. The wild part about it all is that with time and self-reflection, I've come to a place of gratitude that David didn't marry me.

He wasn't fully invested, committed, and in love with every aspect of me and every aspect of my life. And I loved him, all of him. The imbalance was there, and he finally chose to do something about it.

David handled it poorly. There is no denying or changing this fact. He may not see it that way, but it's how I feel. This anger fueled my writing at the start. At first, I wanted him to pay. To know the embarrassment and shame I felt. But deep down, I was desperate to let this anger go once and for all.

No one, not even David, owes me closure. I've found I can have closure on my own. And that's what I'm here to do. I want to own this story that shattered me, bring peace to it, and allow myself to move forward.

As we arrive at the spot, Wes looks quite confused, and I don't blame him.

"You good, hun?" I ask him.

"Yes, but why are we at Costco?" he turns to me. "I thought you said you wanted to visit the spot he ended things? I was prepared for Colorado and have been doing my best to hide the nerves I felt about potentially seeing this guy... But Costco? Really?"

"I know," letting out a nervous laugh, "Believe it or not, this is it. Now come on, follow me." I lead us out of the car to the path that runs along this very public shopping center.

"There are people everywhere, Alice," Wes points out. He's right. It's a very popular path. We continue to pass by families, cyclists, and couples out on a walk.

"Here we are." I stop us under a tree behind Costco. I look out at the stream of water running in front of us. Deep breaths as I take in the details of the surroundings where my life took an unexpected turn. Nothing has changed. Everything around us is the same from that day, but I am completely different.

"Alice, this, this can't be it, how could he—" Wes is getting a little shaken up. For once, I am feeling a little stronger than him when dealing with this story of mine.

If only he knew the girl I was back then. Standing here, begging, and asking for any chance, any sliver of hope for David to change his mind. So unaware of my worth, my value. It hits me just how far I've come.

"Yes, hun, this is the spot," Looking back at him, he's speechless, "Hey, I'm sorry if this is weird for you—"

"No, I'm sorry, I had no idea. How do you end an engagement in public like this?"

"Hey, it's okay, I'm okay. Look at me," I say, holding his hands. "The thing about this experience is that it will always be a part of my life. It's already shaped me more than I thought possible. Plus, it led me to you. On the day David brought me here, I had no idea what was happening. And I left feeling broken, unwanted, kicked to the curb. But now I stand here feeling supported, strong, accepted, and most of all respected."

Wes pulls me in for a long and much needed hug, and I can hear him sniffle. Is he crying now?

"Gah, people probably think we're weird," he says, looking around.

"Wes," cupping his face in my hands, "Sorry to break it to you, babe, but you aren't the first person to cry here."

"You are brilliant. Come here," he pulls me in closer, "Only you could tease yourself like that. In case I haven't told you lately, I love you."

"I know," I say, giving him a kiss, "Now, if you'll let me, I have a letter I would like to read and leave here."

"Go for it. I'm here for you." Wes says as I pull out a folded piece of paper from my back pocket.

Dear David,

You don't know this, but today I stand at the spot where my life changed forever. And the ironic part of it all is that when I met you, I knew you would change my life forever. I felt it in my bones that we were together for a reason. But not in the way I expected.

The last time I was here, you gave me your final goodbye, but I didn't give you mine. I didn't leave expecting that I would never see you again. I thought I would have more time, one more chance, another moment together for closure. You were gone so fast, like an unexpected death. You were stripped and taken away from me, and there was nothing I could do to bring you back. Everything was out of my control, and the person I wanted to be with the most through it all was the reason behind my pain.

The last time I wrote you a letter it was meant for our wedding day. That letter was easy to write. This one isn't.

How you handled everything was inexcusable, and what happened is unfortunately something I will never be able to forget. However, I have fought to get to this place today to make peace with the situation. Your actions may have shown otherwise, but I am choosing to believe your intentions weren't malicious. You saw and felt something off about our future and relationship that I didn't see. It sucked. It wrecked me. And absolutely tore my heart apart. But I'm letting go of that anger today and choosing to thank you.

Because of you and because of what happened, I have found my spirit again and made it even brighter. I am choosing me and the best version of me.

Truth is, it would be easier to list out everything that went wrong with our breakup, but that won't bring me healing or restoration. As challenging as this is, I want to say goodbye with a grateful heart. This story has and will forever continue to shape the woman I am.

So here's to letting go...

Letting go of the resentment.

Letting go of the longing to understand you.

Letting go of the anger.

It's taken me a long time to get to this point because even if I was mad at you, I still had a reason to hold onto you.

But now I'm ready to accept what the world is ready to offer me, and David, I hope you're doing the same.

And lastly, I forgive you.

Wes still has me in my arms as I fold up the letter.

"Alice, wow. How do you feel?"

Letting out a deep breath, I'm shocked I didn't cry.

"I feel free," I say, turning to Wes. "Thank you again for being here with me."

"Of course," he says, holding me tightly.

"Ready?"

"Only if you are, Alice. Take all the time you need."

Grabbing his hand, I lead us back to the car and toss the letter in a trashcan on our way out.

Chapter Twenty-Four

YEAR AND A HALF LATER.

Life is not what I thought it would be—it's better. The past year and a half have been filled with adventure. After declining the initial publishing offer for my tell-all book, I pitched a new idea, and the company loved it. *You're Not Broken,* a book about recovering and coming back from difficult moments in life, specifically broken engagements. I want to inspire readers to know that they aren't defined by a broken relationship, and they can achieve closure on their own. They still kept me on the strict deadline, which meant many late nights typing.

The best part is I was falling deeper in love in the midst of it all.

And starting in a few weeks, I will have a new coffee shop to explore. Wes has ventured into opening another place of his own. It's a little out of the way, somewhere you can only get to through some winding back roads. *Ah,* I can't wait for those scenic drives to lead me to his warm and delicious coffee.

Watching him expand and live out his dream has been so sweet. Together we help each other talk through our ideas for the book or the shop. Wes has become a partner, boyfriend, and best friend all in one. To say I am smitten is an understatement.

Tonight we are going out to celebrate his new business venture and my book release. Even when life is busy, it feels calm with Wes. He is great at keeping us grounded, reminding us to relax and be present. When we aren't working, we are finding and taking on new hobbies. From pickle-ball, to Tuesday night trivia, to game nights with friends, my days are never boring.

As I look in the mirror and add my finishing touches to my look for the night—earrings, lip gloss, a few more spritz of hairspray to combat the Southern humidity—I think about the first time I met Wes. How far we have come. How far I have come. Wes got my attention, but he wasn't a guy who I thought I would or should fall for. I used to have a list of expectations and standards for who I should love. Wes has simply stolen my heart and proven my checkboxes to be outdated.

Knock knock.

"I'll get it!" Chelsea yells out.

Of course, you will, I laugh and mouth to myself. She is still the nosy, too involved roommate. But if it weren't for her letting Wes into the apartment that day he came back for me, he never would have seen the shirt. So in an odd way, I'm thankful for her *curious* spirit.

As I walk out, Wes' eyes meet mine. He slowly looks me up and down before saying a word. The action itself sends chills down my bare legs.

"Look. At. You." Wes makes his way toward me, "Get over here, my goodness, you are a vision."

My face flushes. I did get a new dress for tonight because it felt special, and I always like to look my best for my sweet

Wes. I landed on a mini silk black dress. Light and easy, that is a sophisticated type of sexy. Paired with gold accent jewelry. Hair curled, messy, and up in a ponytail. Wes' favorite look of mine.

Enough about me. He cleaned up well for today. Nice slacks, perfectly fitted, which is an Alice favorite of his. The baggy jeans were sometimes rough for me to accept. But tonight, he is wearing a white button-down, tucked in, sleeves rolled up just enough for a few of his tattoos peek out. Something I never thought I could be fan of in a man but with Wes, it's hot.

"Are you two going to stand here and stare at each other all night or..." Chelsea ends the silent exchanges between us.

Gosh, I forgot she was still standing there.

"Oh Chels, what would we do without you?" I tease without losing eye contact with Wes.

"I ask myself this all the time," she replies.

"All right, shall we?" Wes reaches his arm out to usher me to the door.

"Don't wait up!" I yell back to Chelsea as the door shuts.

*

"And here are the menus. They just arrived today," Wes shares as he hands over a sample.

"Oh wow, so you decided to add some brunch items too?" I ask, scanning the menu.

He asked if we could stop at his restaurant before heading to dinner since I haven't seen the progress in a few weeks. It smells of fresh paint and it's surrounded with lots of windows, just like his original Good & Gather. His eye for creating the perfect amount of natural lighting is unmatched.

"Yes! But take a closer look at the drink selection."

"Oh my gosh, stop it. Weston! You didn't..."

"But I did," he laughs.

"You—you are wild," truly shocked as I read *Alice's Iced Latte* printed in the specialty drinks section.

"Wild about you," he says, pulling the menu away so he can hold my hand. "Which reminds me, this section over here is going to have a nook for readers to sit and enjoy. Thinking it needs about fifty signed copies of your book."

"A nook too? How dreamy!"

"And over here," he adds, pulling me in a new direction, "Imagine a wall of records. Shelves stacked with an eclectic mix of music."

"Wes, it's all so thoughtful. Look at this. Look at you."

"Look at us," he gives my hand a gentle squeeze. "But it still feels like it's missing something."

"Like what? This is amazing! The location is perfect, the vision is—"

"You," Wes responds.

"Me?"

"Yes," his body stiffens, and I can feel his hands getting shaky. "It's missing you."

What is he talking about? I'm here. I am on the menu, for crying out loud.

"I don't understand. I am here. What do you mean?"

"Alice," he continues on before I can question anymore what he means. "When I think about my life, what it is, what I want it to be, I can only picture you beside me."

"Wes—" my hands are shaking now.

Is he about to do what I think he is about to do?

"Alice, when I think about bringing people together, enjoying the present, I want to do that with you. You bring an immense amount of joy and light to areas of my life I didn't realize I needed. The day I met you, my life changed. I saw your strength, your zeal for life, your compassion for others, your contagious and goofy sense of humor, and your killer sense of style. Since that very day, you have continued to take my breath away."

"I love you," I'm barely able to mouth the words as I feel a single tear slip from my eye.

"I love you too. When I started Good & Gather, it was in honor of my dad to bring people together. Little did I know that it would bring me the love of my life, my absolute best friend."

Both of us shaking, standing in the middle of his halfway constructed coffee shop. I feel him let go of one of my hands, and he uses it to reach into his pocket and pull out the little box. Everything becomes a blur as Wes positions himself down on one knee.

"Alice, I promise to be the man who never stops encouraging you, supporting you, loving you, and laughing with you. I will go mad if I wait another minute without making you my wife forever. Alice," he pulls the ring out of the box, "Will you marry me?"

My hands cover my mouth as I nod my head yes. I never thought this moment would come again so easy, but falling in love with Wes was simple, subtle, serene.

"Wes—"

"Is that a yes?" he says, smiling back up at me.

"Yes! Oh my gosh, *yes!*" And with those words, he stands and lifts me into his arms. He swings me around as we delight in this moment.

"Here," he grabs my left hand to put the ring on it.

This ring. It's beautiful. It's massive.

"Wes," I gasp, admiring the emerald-cut diamond on my finger with a simple gold band. "It's stunning!"

"Thanks. I did have a little help."

"I can't believe this. I truly had no idea. My goodness, I love you so much."

"Well, I had some help pulling it all together." He turns toward the kitchen. "You guys can come out now!" Wes shouts.

Suddenly, once again, I am stormed by my people. Mom, Dad, siblings, friends, all here.

"Congrats, Alice. Your fairytale ending!" my mom says as she admires the ring on my finger and gives me a hug.

"Welcome to the family," my dad says, shaking Wes' hand.

Tears, cheers and celebration fill the restaurant as bottles of champagne are popped.

I cannot believe Wes pulled off another surprise for me. When I moved to Nashville, I was trying to prove that I didn't need anyone to move forward and heal from my broken engagement. I was hustling to achieve as much as I could because I thought those accolades were what defined me and made me worthy of love. Wes, my family, and friends have helped me find myself again and have loved me through every up and down. From helping me move around states, witness my heartbreak, cry with me, lift me up and support my dreams, I am reminded what unconditional love feels like. I don't have to earn their love, and they don't have to earn mine.

Love and healing are a choice. And I choose both.

Clinking my glass with the inside of my new ring, I grab the attention of the room, keeping Wes close to my side.

"If I can have everyone's attention." Silence fills the room, and the music is turned low. "I wanted to say thank you to all of you. Today, standing here next to Wes and rejoicing in this sweet sentiment would not be possible had all of you not extended such grace, tenderness, and patience the past couple of years. My gratitude and appreciation stretch well beyond the past few years, and I am so thankful to have the support of you all who have believed in me regardless of the circumstances. Thank you for loving me when others couldn't, thank you for allowing me to always be me, and thank you for helping me find my strength to grow. I love you all."

And with that, the room is once again filled with glasses clinking, laughter, and priceless memories being made.

Life is filled with stories. Difficult, thrilling, unimaginable stories. There isn't a single thing I would do to change my past to keep me from this present.

Owning my story was the best decision I ever made.

Acknowledgments

Writing a book has always been a dream of mine, but I never knew where to start or what to cover. When my world was turned upside down, it would have been easier to stay there, but the people in my life helped me lift myself back up. I said I wanted to turn my story into a book and create a magical ending. Not a single person in my corner shared a doubt. From the bottom of my heart, I want to thank every person who contributed to my campaign, my journey, and my dream. Each of you have planted a seed of hope that helped bring this book across the finish line.

To all the individuals working tirelessly behind the scenes with me, thank you. Specifically to my editors Quinn Karrenbauer and Stephanie McKibben, who pushed me to dig deeper as I turned a personal story into a piece of art. Your guidance and expertise helped me become a stronger writer and embrace the power of vulnerability. To the team and staff at New Degree Press, thank you for welcoming me to your community and providing the tools I needed to blossom as an author.

To all my friends and communities around the world, thank you for your support. It is a gift to have such rich friendships which make the hard times bearable and the good times sweeter. From your care packages, sweet letters, flowers, phone calls, and check-ins, you have helped me find and form my inner spirit. To my Devon, you are the most precious. Thank you for answering every call, encouraging me when I wanted to quit, and accepting me for who I am. You are the greatest best friend a girl could ask for, and I cherish every margarita-filled moment with you. To my Holli, thank you for being the angel I didn't know I needed. You were the light on the darkest day and the spark that inspired me to find my spirit again.

To my family, words can't even express my gratitude. You have helped me at my lowest, celebrated me at my highest, and loved me every moment in between. Our bond as a family is my greatest blessing. To each and every one of my siblings, you inspire me in your own unique ways. Andy, Sarah, JulieAnn, Robert, Mitchell, Kim, Nate, and Lizzie, the compassion and grace all of you have extended will never be forgotten. To my parents, Don and Carla, thank you for teaching me how to persevere through adversity and helping me pick up the pieces. Your level of sacrifice and support are unmatched. Thank you for empowering me to chase after every dream and endeavor and cheering me on every step of the way. I love you all.

And to my grandmother, Alice. The queen of us all. It is an honor to be named after you and have you as a role model in my life. Your adventurous spirit is contagious, your strength is admirable, and your class is impeccable. You embody so many traits that I strive to have and one day pass on to children of my own.

Lastly, to each individual contributor who made this all possible:

Courtney Pagel, Andy Crocker, Sarah Svean, Sarah Crocker, Melissa Russo, Andrew Wood, JulieAnn Ruiz, Robert Ruiz, Chandler Ramirez, Crystal Milinich, Carla Crocker,

Don Crocker, Ralph Rivera, Michelle Ormonde, Alyssa Seifert, Lorene Yost, Ashley Coghill, Jeri Greenberg, Devon Meredith, Talia Van Wingerden, Kelsey Maguire, Karl Flowers, Lauren Wade, Ryan Barry, Gail, Taylor Huerta, Kim Crocker, Mitchell Crocker, Amy Abernathy, Jenna Gordon, Dakota Jackson, Jaleena Evans, Mary Imbach Ramirez, Annie Nanamura, Dakota Himmelman, Brandon Kehoe, Andrew Idell, Tarah Patterson, Santannah Benson, Tomilyn Underwood, Holli McClelland, Stephanie Gwinn, Tamara Lamb, Kelly Ishida, Melanie and Mitchell Petrak, Jane Kisling, Faith Weaver, Carolina Kehoe, Cheryl Jackson, Priscilla Domingo, John Hunt, Wendy Seeley, Alanna Bauman, Brianna Class, Dylan Kelley, Kati Miller, Kayla Rice, Kimberly Janitz, Krista Bayless, Maggie Mosher, Jarred Young, Kari Acosta, Marty Lalanne, Renee Durazo, Julia Rossi, Grant Garry, Alice Reis, Laura Sanford, Eric Koester, Elana Heffley, Meg Ryan, Chrysteen Braun, Kaylee Doyel, Marnie Kavern, Nate Crocker, Luke Hilgenhold, Shane Fisher, Jo Ellen Buckley Mosher, Sue Wright, Jessica Salottolo, Abby Stearns, Brady Baker, Amelia Martin, Katie Huson, Mary Lillin Mills, Lindsey Combest, Taylor Carroll, Kirsten Medice-Wright, Sarah McGlasson, Stephen Ford, Leah Konigsberg, Joyce Leslie, Joe & Kathiann Crocker, Lucy Mosher, Mary Bowman, Vanessa LaFollette, Allisyn Pugh, Heidi Cougoule, Kaley Roberts, Ania Spann, Amanda Kaye, Cam Adams, Kacie Pechota, Ashley O'Hearn, Elizabeth Crocker, Rachel Rountree, Renu Linberg, Steven Alba, Tracy Cherry, Kathy Ruiz, Neva Ruso, April Hopkins, Julianne Buckley, Kayla Hines, Jessica Berengut, Louise Millet, Ashley Whalen, Sydney Mueller, Maile Osumi, Kami Nanamura, Electa Wright, Nancy Scheck, Isabel LoBue, Dionisia Riviere, Connor Yost, Asia Martinez, Amanda Shoultz, Blain Smothermon, Ann Andreini, Bailey

Wineman, Megan Stephens, Mary Burns, Ciara Holt, Kymmber Davidson, Payton Cherry, Elizabeth Jacobs, Kalen Kools, Taylor Peterson, Amy Hunt, Kyla Conway, Julie Enos, Olivia Steinfeld, Camryn Berra, Hailey Smothermon, Brooke Baumgardner, Catherine Buckley

To every person who has helped keep me steady and allowed me to be me, thank you.

Made in the USA
Las Vegas, NV
31 January 2022

42692085R00134